D0567382

America Goes to War

AMERICA GOES TO WAR

1941

John Devaney

Walker and Company
New York

This book is dedicated to Robert Scott, who
died at Pearl Harbor on December 7, 1941,
and to the thousands of other men and women
who gave their lives in 1941 fighting
for the Four Freedoms.

First published in the United States of America in 1991
by Walker Publishing Company, Inc.

Published simultaneously in Canada by
Thomas Allen & Son
Canada, Limited, Markham, Ontario

Library of Congress Cataloging-in-Publication Data
Devaney, John.
America goes to war: 1941 / by John Devaney.
p. cm.
Includes bibliographical references and index.
Summary: Uses brief personal vignettes to pinpoint dramatic and
significant events, concerning both political figures and ordinary
people, during the first year of America's involvement in World War
II.
ISBN 0-8027-6979-9   ISBN 0-8027-6980-2 (lib. bdg.)
1. World War, 1939–1945—United States—Juvenile literature.
2. United States—History—1933–1945—Juvenile literature.
3. World War, 1939–1945—Juvenile literature.   [1. World War, 1939–1945.]
I. Title.
D769.D48   1991
940.53'73—dc20   90-41739
CIP
AC

Printed in the United States of America

1 2 3 4 5 6 7 8 9 10

PROLOGUE

AUGUST 31, 1939–DECEMBER 31, 1940

The German storm trooper saw the radio station's tower etched against the moonlit sky. He crawled closer to the station, dragging a man dressed in the uniform of a Polish soldier.

He signaled to two other storm troopers. They also dragged men wearing Polish uniforms. The men had been prisoners in a German concentration camp. They had been drugged, dressed in Polish uniforms, thrown into a truck, and driven to this German radio station on the border between Germany and Poland.

It was almost eight o'clock on this cool night of August 31, 1939. The SS men set up machine guns. Moments later, the guns blasted a stream of bullets that flew harmlessly past the radio station building. The SS men then pulled out pistols, shot the three prisoners, and slipped away into the darkness, leaving the corpses strewn on the radio station's lawn.

Minutes later, Adolf Hitler's Nazi government announced to the world that Polish troops had attacked a German radio station. German cameramen photographed the corpses, Hitler's "proof" that Poland—not Germany—had made the first move. Hitler declared war on Poland and nine hours later, at 4:45 on the morning of September 1, 1939, fifty-three divisions of German troops—more than a million and a half men—crossed the border into Poland.

Led by tanks and diving Stuka bombers, Hitler's army swarmed over Poland's twenty-three divisions. His Luftwaffe fighters blew Poland's old planes out of the sky. The Polish army reeled back eastward toward the capital of Warsaw.

Great Britain and France had pledged to go to war if Poland were attacked. Both nations declared war on Germany. British troops streamed across the English Channel to join the French. One hundred and fifty Allied French and British divisions faced the Germans on the French-German border. They outnumbered the Germans six to one. The bulk of Hitler's troops had been sent eastward to smash Poland.

If the British and French attacked, German generals told each other, the Allied army would pierce the weakened German line and jab its way to Germany's heart. World War II would be over in days. But the French and British did not attack. They sat behind the forts of the Maginot Line. Hitler had gambled that the Allies lacked the heart to attack. He won the gamble.

Hitler's bombers slaughtered Warsaw's

helpless civilians until the Poles surrendered. The war was over in a month.

As Poland collapsed, Soviet Russian dictator Josef Stalin swept into Poland from the east. His armies occupied Poland's rich farmlands. Like Hitler, Stalin wanted more of everything — more food, more ports to his north, more oil to his south. Both dictators knew that ships, food, and oil strengthened the war machines that increased a nation's power.

Hitler and his storm troopers led Germany into World War II. The Nazi salute, demonstrated here by the mustached Hitler, was followed with the words "Heil Hitler!" When up to a half-million Germans thundered those words at mass ceremonies like this one, people around the world listened on radio, and shuddered. *(National Archives)*

Hitler and Stalin had signed a peace treaty that divided Europe into halves — Eastern Europe ruled by Russia, Western Europe by Germany.

Hitler now turned his back on the east to conquer the west. By April of 1940, his troops had landed in Norway. The British had sent troops, battleships, and planes to aid the Norwegians, but they came, many Americans said, with too little too late. By June, the battered British had to escape by sea.

Hitler stood as the master of all northern Europe.

His tank-led troops, meanwhile, had launched his blitzkrieg—"lightning war"—against the French and British. His armored columns juggernauted through Belgium and Holland, then knifed into the exposed flanks of the French and British armies, still sitting behind the Maginot Line. Belgium and Holland quickly surrendered. Hitler's fast tanks shot between the Allied armies, encircling almost two million troops.

The bloodied remnants of the Allied army—fewer than 500,000 men—staggered backward to the English Channel. They huddled on a stretch of sandy beach at Dunkirk, France. Nazi tanks and troops massed to drive the stunned Allies into the sea. Thousands of English vessels—corvettes, destroyers, fishing boats, even men, women, and teenagers in their own small motorboats—churned across the Channel to try to rescue the trapped soldiers. British admirals had hoped to save perhaps 50,000 soldiers. Instead, more than 338,000 British and French soldiers scrambled aboard the boats that ferried them in a near-miracle escape to England.

The bloodied, exhausted Allied soldiers and sailors were met by a new British leader, the ruddy-faced, plump Winston Churchill. Speaking on radio, he promised a worldwide audience listening on shortwave radio, "We shall defend our island no matter what the cost may be. We shall fight on the beaches, on the landing grounds, in the fields, in the streets and in the hills." Then, thrilling the world with the defiance of his words, he said, "We shall never surrender!"

But that struggle, he knew, would be a long and painful one. He told the British people: "I have nothing to offer you but blood, toil, tears, and sweat."

In Berlin Adolf Hitler, his piercing blue eyes seeming to stare through the sheafs of paper, studied Sea Lion, his plan to invade England in September. He met with Italy's dictator, the bull-chested Benito Mussolini. He approved a thrust by Italian troops across North Africa to capture British-owned Egypt and the Suez Canal. Victory in North Africa by Germany and Italy—the Axis powers—would cut off England from its colonies, India, Australia, and New Zealand, which were sending arms, troops, and food. It would also open up all of Africa's vast land and riches to the two dictators.

Early in September, Hitler added a third power—Japan—to the Axis powers. Germany, Italy, and Japan signed a treaty promising to attack any nation that attacked any one of them. That, gloated Hitler, would keep the United States from rushing to the aid of England. If the United States sided with England, Japan's navy could attack America's battlewagons in the Pacific.

Japan's army had invaded the vastness of China, seeking what Hitler and Mussolini sought—more land and more food. The Chinese, led by Generalissimo Chiang Kai-shek and his Communist army allies, had kept Japanese troops bogged down in China.

Japan now looked for easier and richer prey. Its military rulers hungered for Britain's India and other colonies of Southeast Asia owned by the vanquished French and Dutch. The colonies were vast and filled with the raw materials that Japan need for its factories and the food it needed for its growing millions of people. But the United States president, Franklin Roosevelt, had warned Japan that it was wrong for one nation to grab the wealth of a defeated one.

Americans, meanwhile, argued loudly over whether the United States should send food

Isolationists, picketing in front of the British Embassy in Washington, in 1941 opposed Roosevelt's intervening to help Great Britain. Many Americans felt they had been "suckered" into World War I to help save France and England from Germany. They argued that America shouldn't make the same mistake twice. (© Washington Post; *reprinted by permission of the Washington, D.C., Public Library*)

and weapons to England. Some Americans, called interventionists, said yes. Hitler, they said, would smash America if he destroyed England. Other Americans, called isolationists, said that the Atlantic Ocean stretched too wide for Germany to cross. Let's mind our own business, they said, and steer clear of Europe's bloody wars.

The summer of 1940 turned to autumn; World War II was now a year old. German submarines prowled the Atlantic, torpedoing ships bringing food from North and South America. The English had to ration food—each person, for example, got one egg a month.

Hitler was winning the Battle of the Atlantic. His Luftwaffe planes roared across the Channel—the Battle of Britain had now begun. German fighters zoomed out of the sun's glare to wipe the skies clear of the Royal Air Force planes. Hitler's troops could then cruise over the Channel with no fear of being strafed by British fighters. German bombers shook London and other British cities, leaving behind blazing bonfires a mile high. Hitler hoped to frighten British men, women, and children so they would surrender.

By now the RAF could send aloft fewer than 2,000 pilots to dogfight German planes that outnumbered them four to one. The RAF pilots rose in their Hurricanes and Spitfires to see Heinkels and Messerschmitts rush toward them in waves that stretched as far back as France thirty miles away.

As the new year, 1941, began, the thin line of RAF pilots stood as the only fighting force holding off Hitler's final triumph in Europe. Many were teenagers, and the others were mostly below twenty-five. Speaking of the brave young aviators, Churchill told the world, "Never in the field of human conflict have so many owed so much to so few."

Chapter One

JANUARY 1 TO 3: *Biggin Hill, an RAF fighter base near London*

The broad-shouldered, trench-coated American war correspondent Quentin Reynolds watched the young RAF pilots kicking the soccer ball. The goalie stood in front of a low-slung Spitfire. The other pilots tried to boot the ball under the fighter's fuselage. The squadron's eleven other Spitfires were clustered at one end of the landing field.

One of the pilots left the soccer game and trotted over to Reynolds. He said his name was Douglas. "Would you like to know how a Spitfire works?" Douglas asked.

Douglas gave the heavyset Reynolds a boost with his shoulder to help him into the narrow cockpit. "You hold that little wheel in front of you with your right hand to steer the aircraft," Douglas said. "You hold the throttle with your left hand to slow down or speed up. See that little button on the wheel? You press that to fire the six machine guns mounted on your wings."

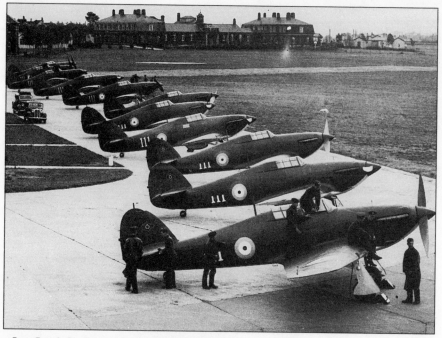

At a Royal Air Force base in England, crewmen check out a squadron of Hurricane fighters. Hurricanes and Spitfires were being lost faster than England could build them as the Germans had bombed the airplane factories. If Hitler had kept up the bombings, the Battle of Britain might have been lost. But, angered by a British raid over Berlin, he instead ordered his Luftwaffe to attack English cities, ignoring the factories. *(National Archives)*

Reynolds saw what looked like an automobile's rearview mirror mounted on the thick glass windshield of the cockpit. "You always want to look at that mirror," Douglas said, "to make sure there's nobody sitting on your tail."

A field telephone rang. The squadron commander picked it up on the third ring. He listened a few seconds, slammed down the phone, and shouted, "A scramble! Messerschmitts and Heinkels coming in over the Channel at fourteen-thousand feet."

The pilots jerked on leather helmets that covered their faces except the nose and eyes. They buckled on their packed chutes, slung low on their backs and so heavy that they had to duck-waddle toward their planes. Inside the cockpits they stuck small white discs into their mouths, microphones to talk to each other by radio.

In three-abreast lines, the Spitfires jounced down the field, trailing clouds of dust. They lifted into the air, assembled in V-shaped formations of three, then flew toward the Channel at 16,000 feet on a sunny, cloudless day.

"Tally-ho! Tally-ho! There they are!" the squadron commander's voice crackled into helmeted earphones.

Looking down at the frothy Channel, Douglas saw the cigarlike fuselage of a Heinkel 2,000 feet below him. He kicked his right rudder, banked, and dived. His thumb near the firing button, he moved a lever from "safety" to "fire." He looked through the aiming sight—a red circle with two lines that crisscrossed. Now plunging straight down at the bomber, he hoped the Heinkel's gunners hadn't seen him. His thumb tensed over the firing button as he waited for the Heinkel to fill the circle.

"You'd better look behind you! You'd better look behind you!"

It was the warning voice of Sergeant Isaacs, buzzing above him. Douglas glanced at his rearview mirror and saw an Me-110 snapping at his tail. He kicked the rudder, swerved left away from the Heinkel, and began a vertical climb. The Me-110 zoomed by, guns blazing at empty air.

Douglas's Spitfire clawed upward to get above the dogfights swirling around him. He saw two fighters tailing Isaacs.

"So had you! So had you!" he screamed—too late. Isaacs's Spitfire belched red and blue flames from under its cowling. It banked slowly, then streaked downward, wrapped in flames.

Douglas saw Isaacs's Spitfire disappear into clouds. He looked at his rearview. Nothing. The Messerschmitts had run out of fuel. Like the Spitfires, they could stay up for no more than an hour and a half. The Heinkels turned tail for home, splashing their bombs harmlessly into the Channel.

Minutes later, the Spitfire squadron bumped down onto the field at Biggin. The squadron leader asked, "Where's Isaacs?"

"I saw him go down," Douglas said quietly.

Quentin Reynolds came back two days later to talk to the squadron. Pointing to a reedlike pilot, the squadron leader said to Reynolds, "You'll recognize his accent."

"The name is Art Donahue," the pilot said.

"And you're from Texas," Reynolds said, immediately recognizing the soft drawl.

"From Laredo," Donahue said. He was one of hundreds of volunteers from the United States, Canada, and other nations who had joined the RAF. Of the RAF's 3,000 pilots, 500 were from Eire across the Irish Channel. One of those Irish pilots, Brendan (Paddy) Finucaine, had shot down more Germans than any other RAF ace.

The field phone rang once, twice, the fateful third time. "A scramble! A scramble!"

The pilots waddled to their Spitfires. Reynolds gave Douglas a foot up into the cockpit.

"Good luck," Reynolds said to his new RAF pal.

The blue-eyed Douglas grinned back and said, "I might need it this time."

Two days later, Quentin Reynolds typed this last paragraph of his story, which he cabled to *Collier's* magazine in New York: "I guess he needed more luck than I had to give him. Fifteen minutes later the boy was dead."

JANUARY 4: *Washington, the White House*

President Roosevelt sat in a wheelchair. His withered legs had been paralyzed years earlier by an attack of infantile paralysis. His legs now held rigid by iron braces, the President could stand but he couldn't walk without help. Neither braces nor a wheelchair nor a glum, wintry day could wipe away the grin that was nearly always on his large face. He delighted in telling stories that puzzled his listeners.

"Suppose my neighbor's home catches on fire," he told two visitors. "If I loaned him a garden hose to quench the fire," the President said, "would I expect him to pay me the fifteen dollars that the hose cost? Of course not! He would just want his garden hose returned."

The President laughed. Did the visitors

know what he meant? No, they said. You soon will, Roosevelt said.

A few days earlier, the President had spoken on radio during one of his "Fireside Chats" to the nation. "Never before," he said, "has our civilization been in such danger as now. If Great Britain goes down . . . all of us in the Americas could be living at the point of a gun." America, said Roosevelt, had to become "the great arsenal of democracy." Great Britain needed help from that arsenal—guns, planes, and warships, for example—but it didn't have the money to pay for that help.

JAN. 5: *The Atlantic Ocean, off the Scottish coast*

This was twenty-year-old Younger Wood's first trip across the Atlantic as a third mate. At seventeen, he had left a Liverpool school to be a sailor on cargo ships. When war started, Younger went to maritime school and got his ticket as a third mate. He signed aboard a tanker that was now filled with oil from Texas. The tanker lumbered through the midnight darkness toward England.

Younger slippled into his bunk, just relieved of his 8 P.M.-to-midnight watch. The torpedo's explosion threw him out of his bunk, splinters of wood raining down on his face. He climbed a ladder to the deck. Star shells lit up the night as the convoy's zigzagging destroyers searched for the submarine that had torpedoed the tanker and two other cargo ships.

On the bridge Younger saw the pale faces of the first mate and the captain. A deafening crack shook the bridge. Hunks of metal showered around the three officers. The first mate crashed to the deck, his forehead gushing blood. Younger helped him to his feet.

The captain ordered Younger and the first mate to take one of the two lifeboats being lowered by crewmen. "A greaser is missing," a sailor shouted.

Greasers worked in the engine room. His heart pounding, Younger ran down a ladder to the engine room. He saw no one. He climbed up the ladder. A blast of heat suddenly seared his back. Tongues of flame leaped at him from the engine room.

The lifeboat was already in the water, tossing in the dark swells. Younger dived into the frigid water and swam to the boat. Arms pulled him inside. He shook with cold and fright.

The tanker's stern rose slowly in the water. Its bow plunged straight down into the ocean, sending waves that cascaded over the lifeboat, drenching its forty-nine passengers. Spitting out salt water and half blinded, the men grabbed buckets to bail out the water that half filled the small boat.

They rode the boat eastward into a misty dawn. "Ship on port quarter," a voice shouted. Heads swiveled toward a smudge of smoke on the horizon. But then the smoke faded. The shivering men saw nothing but a tossing ocean and a gray sky. The seventeen-year-old radio-man began to sob.

Near three that afternoon, the men saw another smudge—and this smudge moved closer and closer. Just before sunset, the forty-nine survivors climbed aboard their rescuer, a Canadian corvette. A sailor on the corvette said to Younger, "You are the lucky ones. I hate to think of all the little boats out there that we never find."

JAN. 6: *Washington, the Congress of the United States*
The congressmen stood to applaud the President as he began his State of the Union speech. Franklin Delano Roosevelt had become the first president to be elected to a third term.

A British tanker sinks in the North Atlantic after being torpedoed by a German U-boat. The crew of this ship was lucky; she sank slowly. Often a torpedo would set off explosions that incinerated ship and crew within seconds amid one big ball of white flame. *(National Archives)*

Running for reelection last fall, he had promised American mothers: "I have said this before, but I shall say it again and again. Your boys are not going to be sent into any foreign wars."

Roosevelt now asked Congress to pass what would be called the Lend-Lease Law. That law would allow the president to lend or lease guns, tanks, planes, and ships to any nation that the president thought needed help. That country, every American knew, was the neighbor whose house was on fire—England.

"Such aid is not an act of war," the President said. "When the dictators are ready to make war upon us, they will not wait for an act of war on our part. They didn't wait for Norway or Belgium or the Netherlands to commit an act of war." Victory over the dictators, he added, would make the world a place "founded upon four essential freedoms—freedom of speech, freedom of religion, freedom from want, and freedom from fear—everywhere in the world."

Meanwhile, said the President, the United States must arm itself. In 1938, the United States Army numbered only 200,000 men—a dwarf next to Hitler's three-million-man army. America's new Selective Service law had drafted hundreds of thousands of men into the Army for a year of training. Soon, said the President, the Army would number one million men.

The President said he proposed to spend $11 billion of the nation's $17 billion budget in 1941 on defense. He wanted to build 50,000 bombers and fighters a year for the Army's Air Corps. He wanted to launch enough battleships and aircraft carriers so that the U.S. Navy's guns would rule over both the Atlantic and Pacific oceans.

Republicans and Democrats applauded when the President asked for more money for defense. But the Lend-Lease bill, they said, would make Roosevelt a military dictator. "Lend-Lease," said Ohio Republican senator Robert Taft, "authorizes the President to declare war on any nation in the world." Isolationists like Taft and Montana senator Burton Wheeler said that Roosevelt wanted to use Lend-Lease to send American soldiers to die for England.

JANUARY 8: *Berchtesgaden, Germany*

A dolf Hitler paced up and down the long living room. His piercing eyes stared through the picture window of the Berghof. This was Hitler's vacation home, a white-and-green-shuttered mansion perched on a cliff high above the snow-covered Bavarian mountains. Two of his chief military officers, Admiral Eric Raeder and General Fritz Halder, sat on chairs as Hitler reread a message from Josef Stalin.

The Russian dictator was demanding more land in Eastern Europe. And he wanted oil fields in the Balkans of southern Europe—oil that Hitler also thirsted to grab. "Stalin demands more and more," Hitler ranted. "He's a cold-blooded blackmailer. A German victory is becoming unbearable for Russia. Therefore, she must be brought to her knees as soon as possible."

He paused to glare out the picture window, then spoke more calmly and thoughtfully.

"If the United States and Russia should enter the war against Germany," Hitler went on as Halder scribbled notes for his diary, "that would not be [good for Germany]. But it will take America four or five years to arm herself so she would be strong enough to attack Germany. . . . If Russia is defeated, that would free Japan to turn and be a danger to the United States, keeping America out of our war with Britain."

Hitler turned and nodded to Halder. The general knew what the nod meant. Operation Sea Lion—the invasion of England—was postponed. Preparations for Operation Barbarossa—the invasion of Russia—should begin at once.

JANUARY 10: *London, 10 Downing Street*

Harry Hopkins walked into the Prime Minister's office and shook hands with Winston Churchill. Hopkins had landed in London after flying from New York on a Pan-American Clipper flying boat. Hopkins was President Roosevelt's right-hand man. No one was closer to the President's ear than Harry Hopkins.

Dressed in a dirty tan raincoat and a beat-up fedora that slouched over his eyes, the keen-eyed Hopkins had walked London's streets. He had seen gaunt and hungry faces, children crying for food. The British, he wrote in his diary, were losing perhaps their last battle—the battle of the Atlantic.

Hopkins sat down with Churchill and saw in the ruddy face the look of a man searching for a morsel of good news. Hopkins gave him more than a morsel.

"The President is determined that we will win the war together," Hopkins said. "Make no mistake about it. He has sent me here to tell you that at all costs and by all means he will carry you through. . . . There is nothing he will not do. . . ." And later he added, quoting Scripture: "Thy people shall be my people . . . even to the end." Churchill began to weep, and his personal physican, Lord Moran, later told why: "The words seemed like a rope thrown to a drowning man."

JANUARY 12: *Princeton, New Jersey*

As the debate began in the Congress on passing or rejecting the Lend-Lease bill, a Gallup poll announced that 60 percent of Americans were in favor of some kind of aid to

England. But only 12 percent favored going to war.

JANUARY 12: *Hiroshima Bay, Japan*

In his cabin aboard the battleship *Nagato*, the short, thick-chested admiral wrote feverishly. He was Isoroku Yamamoto, commander of all Japanese fleets. He was rewriting a letter he had been composing in his mind for months.

Yamamoto knew that Japan's politicians would talk the Emperor into invading Southeast Asia. Yamamoto believed that the United States would go to war to stop Japan's thrust southward. He had attended Harvard. He knew America's immense strength, its industrial power. In a long war, he told himself, America would defeat Japan. But it was his duty to fight that coming war with all of his skill and cunning.

Japan's war plan called for its navy to land a million soldiers in Southeast Asia. Japan's admirals hoped that the American navy would leave its Pearl Harbor base in the mid-Pacific to attack the Japanese navy off Asia. The American ships would run out of fuel and shells and float helplessly some 5,000 miles from home. Japanese guns would blow the Americans out of the water. Japan would rule the Pacific. The Americans would be thrown back onto their continent and Japan would do what it wanted in the Pacific and in Asia. Or so the Japanese daydreamed.

Yamamoto knew the Americans would not be lured so far from Pearl Harbor. He had a better plan. Why not attack and destroy the American Pacific Fleet as it slept at rest in what it thought was the safety of Pearl Harbor?

Yamamoto knew that Japan's real rulers, generals and admirals, would call the plan too risky. How could the navy sneak close enough to attack Pearl Harbor without being spotted and destroyed? Impossible!

But Admiral Yamamoto had a reputation in the navy. Somehow he always got his way.

JANUARY 16: *New York City, Radio City*

The lean, wiry billionaire Joseph P. Kennedy had just returned from London, where he had served as the U.S. Ambassador to Great Britain. He was convinced that Hitler would destroy the British. He had told Roosevelt that sending more aid to Great Britain would be "money down the drain."

Isolationists had asked Kennedy to deliver a nationwide radio speech telling Congress to reject the Lend-Lease bill. "If I could be assured," he told millions of listeners, "that America could . . . end the threat of German domination, I would be in favor of declaring war right now. [But] we are not prepared to fight a war— even a defensive one."

Then he gave a favorite argument of isolationists. "For the life of me," he said, "I can't understand why the talk of a great military

machine like Hitler's, which is three thousand miles away, should make us fear for our security. It is impossible for us to invade Europe, just as it is impossible for Germany to invade us."

Ambassador Joseph Kennedy flanked by his two oldest sons, Joseph (right) and John, just after his return from England. John (the family called him Jack) was writing a book, *While England Slept,* about how England had been fooled by Hitler during the 1930s. Joe, the oldest son, was considered the brightest by the family. The Kennedys talked about one day seeing him in the White House. He was killed when his bomber exploded later in the war. *(National Archives)*

After finishing the speech, Kennedy posed for photographers with two of his sons, Joe and Jack.

Listening to the speech at his family home at Hyde Park, New York, high above the Hudson River, President Roosevelt had to wince. He knew that Kennedy's speech, his money, and his influence would build votes in Congress against Lend-Lease. If Lend-Lease lost, he told his aides, Hitler would win this war and at least half the world.

JANUARY 19: *Puch, Germany*

The heavy-jawed Benito Mussolini walked off the train and saw Hitler waiting for him on the platform. Mussolini's Italian army in North Africa had invaded Egypt, but the British army had pushed the Italians back into Libya, where the Italians had started their attack.

And there was more bad news. A month earlier, Mussolini had decided to attack his neighbor, Greece, without telling Hitler. Here, too, there was defeat. The Greeks knocked the Italians back to their bases in Albania.

The usually jaunty Mussolini shuffled sheepishly toward Hitler. He had come to the Berghof to beg for Hitler's help in Greece and North Africa.

Hitler shook Mussolini's hand. It would do no good to scold Il Duce, as Mussolini was called. Hitler wanted England and America to think no Axis power could be defeated anywhere. He would have to pull Mussolini's armies out of the fire in Greece and Africa.

Homeless children sit in front of their wrecked house. German bombers hit London's docks in the East End, where most of the poor lived. Agitators screamed that the wealthy in London had made deals with the Germans to be spared during the blitzes of 1940 and 1941—but the protests died down when a bomb hit in front of Buckingham Palace, home of the King and Queen. *(National Archives)*

JANUARY 25: *London, the East End*

B omb craters pockmarked the streets. Cardboard and old newspapers covered the shattered windows of the old buildings in this neighborhood of the poor. The winter's wind whipped through holes in bomb-torn houses to leave icicles on bathroom faucets. Hitler's blitz had killed more than 20,000 men, women, and children and injured more than 40,000.

Bus drivers refused to drive during air raids. Millions of bomb-shocked workers slept during the day, too exhausted to work. Most people had the energy to work only three hours a day. More than half the people thought the war would never end. Victory would come, most Britons thought, only if the United States and Russia joined the war against Hitler—and that, they also thought, was unlikely.

Chapter Two

FEBRUARY 2: *Detroit, Cadillac Square*

Sixteen-year-old Alice Ann Ritchie and her bobby-soxer friends were laughing almost hysterically. They pushed Anesthesia one more time. Anesthesia was a fifteen-year-old Ford that Alice and her girlfriends had bought for thirty dollars. The car lived up to its sleepy name. After two hours of bowling, the girls had to push the jalopy to get it started.

Alice wore the brown and white saddle shoes and the chunky white ankle-length "bobby" socks that had given a generation of girls a label. Bobby-soxers' skirts came just to their knees. Fluffy blue or pink angora sweaters and shoulder-length hairdos—like Vivien Leigh's as Scarlett O'Hara in *Gone With the Wind*—were the fashion.

Boys wore saddle shoes or high-top rubber-soled sneakers. Most high school principals demanded that they wear ties with a jacket or sweater. Just out of knee-length knickers, boys worked and played in blue denim pants they called dungarees.

Alice and her friends dated on Saturday nights. Dates and double dates went together to a neighborhood movie, then to a drugstore or ice-cream parlor for fifteen-cent sundaes. Favorite movie stars were Errol Flynn, Clark Gable, teenage singers Deanna Durbin and Judy Garland, and Mickey Rooney, who played an impish teenager named Andy Hardy. Some girls liked to write to a new movie star—the boyish-faced Ronald Reagan.

Teenagers had a language all their own. If you liked something, you said, "That's solid." If you didn't like somebody, you said, "You're a droop." "B.U.," or "smooching," or "gooing it," meant kissing. If you enjoyed something, it was "copacetic."

On Sunday nights, the kids stretched out on the living-room floor to do their homework and listen to the radio comedy shows—Jack Benny, Fred Allen, or Charlie McCarthy. During the week, the family turned on the evening news. They heard Gabriel Heatter begin each radio

Bobby-soxers chatting before classes at a Baltimore high school. A boy who was "icky" was to be avoided, but if a boy was "groovy" girls wanted to date him. The two girls in the middle are wearing what most every teenage girl—and many boys—owned: brown and white saddle shoes. (*Library of Congress*)

broadcast with "There's good news tonight"—
even when there was only bad news. In the after-
noons, mothers and their daughters listened to
soap operas like "The Romance of Helen Trent"
and "Our Gal Sunday." Boys liked adventure and
western shows: Jack Armstrong, the All-Ameri-
can Boy, and the Lone Ranger. Later at night,
high school seniors tuned in the big bands playing
at hotels in New York, Chicago, or San Francisco.
In their bedrooms, they silently practiced the steps
of the Lindy Hop while listening to Benny Good-
man play "Don't Be That Way" or hear Glenn
Miller blast "Tuxedo Junction."

Fathers talked about buying one of the new
fluid-drive cars—"You can drive for hours,"
said the ads, "without shifting." But the price
was high for people making $25 or $30 a week.
The new fluid-drive Dodge cost about $900.

People had more money in their pockets
than at any time since before the Great Depression had paralyzed American in 1930. Only five
years before, about one of every five Americans
did not have a job. Now nine out of ten had
jobs. But everything had become so expensive.
Beef had shot up to 32 cents a pound and eggs
cost 21 cents a dozen. You couldn't buy a de-
cent suit for under $25, and winter dresses cost
as much as $24. Shoes were $6.50 to $20 a pair.

Houses were also expensive—as much as
$5,000 for a new three-bedroom home. And
you had to put $500 down, more than most
Americans had in their bank accounts.

FEBRUARY 10: *Sag Harbor, New York*

The students at Pierson High School decided to celebrate Bill of Rights Week by learning what life would be like in a dictatorship. Two of the dictator's "spies" were planted in each class. During the day, offenders were reported to the "secret police" for wearing lipstick, writing letters, meeting in groups. Punishment came swiftly. The secret police herded offenders out of the building. With clubs over their heads, girls and boys scrubbed sidewalks on their knees.

At 3 P.M., the announcement over loudspeakers—"Dictatorship Day is over"—was greeted with cheers. The students massed in the auditorium to sing the song that radio's Kate Smith had made popular—"God Bless America."

Kids talked about Dictatorship Day that afternoon in the soda parlor on Main Street. They put nickels into the jukebox to play Tommy Dorsey's new hit, "I'll Never Smile Again." The girls listened carefully when Dorsey's new singer joined the chorus. They said they could swoon over Frank Sinatra.

Frank Sinatra chats with three members of his fan club. He had been singing with two big bands for almost five years—first with Harry James, now with Tommy Dorsey—and he was thinking of becoming a singer on his own. *(From the author's collection)*

FEBRUARY 12: *Washington, Capitol Hill*

B urton Wheeler told reporters that the Air
Corps had only 636 planes, not one of
them the equal of a Messerschmitt-110 or a
Spitfire. Of the 2,884 military planes that rolled
out of U.S. factories in 1940, he said, "an
astounding 2,308 went to England and other
countries, a bare 576 to the United States
Army."

Reporters asked President Roosevelt to com-
ment. "Such secret military figures," the President said in his poker-faced way, "must be sat-
isfying for Reich Chancellor Hitler."

FEBRUARY 12: *London, 10 Downing Street*

C hurchill was writing a cable to General Ar-
chibald Wavell, the commander of the
British Army of the Nile in North Africa. Wavell's army had swept the Italians out of Egypt
and crashed across 500 miles of Libyan desert,
capturing 130,000 Italians.

"Accept my heartfelt congratulations,"
Churchill cabled, ". . . on the unexpected speed
with which [Libya] has been conquered."

Then Churchill turned to what was tops on
his mind in the Mediterranean war. Known
only to Churchill and a handful of British generals, the British code breakers had perfected a
code-breaking machine, called Ultra. Every order sent by Hitler to his generals was being read
by Ultra's code breakers in London. Ultra had
told Churchill that Hitler planned to aid Mussolini by smashing Greece.

"Our first thoughts must be for our ally Greece," Churchill cabled Wavell. If Hitler conquered Greece, Hitler would stand only a few hundred miles across from Turkey. Hitler would bully Turkey into standing aside and allowing his legions to sweep into the Middle East with its rich oil fields of Iraq and Syria.

Be ready, Churchill told Wavell, to move most of the Army of the Nile to Greece.

Churchill had another reason for blocking Hitler's plunge into Greece. That reason was America. "Any loss of Greece would be very harmful on American public opinion," he told Anthony Eden, his foreign minister.

Eden had flown to Athens to convince Greek officials that they should allow British troops to enter their country if Hitler attacked. The Greeks feared the help would be too little and too late—and would only get Hitler madder at them. But Churchill was anxious to send troops so that Americans like Kennedy could not charge that Britain had lost another battle because of "too little too late."

FEBRUARY 16: *New Orleans, a recruiting center*

Mrs. L. M. Joffrion, of nearby Donaldsville, came to the center with her three oldest sons, Leonard, twenty, Ray, eighteen, and Olin, seventeen. They were being sworn into the U.S. Army Air Corps. Her husband, now dead, had fought in France during World War I.

"When they were babies," she told a *Times-Picayune* reporter, "I kept hoping I wasn't bringing them up to fight. But, well, it looks like I am. I think the best way of staying out of war is by being fully prepared. I'm not in favor of fighting a war on foreign soil, but if that becomes necessary, it's something that has to be done."

FEBRUARY 23: *Athens, Greek Ministry of Foreign Affairs*

After round-the-clock meetings, General Wavell and Anthony Eden signed an agreement with the Greek government. The British promised to send 100,000 troops to Greece to help fight any invasion by Germany.

FEBRUARY 24: *Washington, the U.S. Senate*

Nevada's Pat McCarran rose to speak against Lend-Lease. "If this bill is passed," said the slender senator, "every boy who goes into the Army next month will be going for good. He may think he's going for a year—that's the happy promise—but he is going out to die."

FEBRUARY 25: *Tripoli, Libya*

General Erwin Rommel watched the seventeen-ton Mark IV Panzer tanks rumble down the ancient, cobbled streets. He had come to North Africa to take command of the shattered Italian armies. Thousands of German sol-

diers streamed into Tripoli. Rommel was form-
ing a new army—the Afrika Korps.

The tanks—the Korps had only fifty—as-
sembled in front of Rommel. His generals ad-
vanced and saluted. Spies had told Rommel that
much of the Army of the Nile was sailing to
Greece. "We're going to advance through
Libya into Egypt," Rommel told his generals.
"We're going to roll to Cairo and the Suez
Canal."

FEBRUARY 28: *Oklahoma City*

Mrs. D. V. Clark, the mother of Ezell
"Bud" Orbison, received a letter from
her son in England. He was one of more than a
hundred American pilots who had volunteered
to join the RAF's American Eagle Squadron.
"Please don't worry about me, because I'm going to do something I like," her son wrote.
"I'm going to be a part of something important
during my life, and this is the best way to do
it." Two days earlier, Mrs. Clark had been no-
tified that her son was dead, the third American
pilot to die in the Battle of Britain.

Chapter Three

MARCH 6: *New York*

I n the new issue of *Time* magazine, Americans read under "Foreign News":

". . . Hitler has taught the Jews in the Third Reich . . . the misery of subtraction. From all of them he has taken something: privileges, property, home, life. . . . Hitler's final solution to his problem in subtraction is zero."

MARCH 6: *Lorient, France*

F rom outside the windows, the Three Aces could hear the laughter of their submarine crews enjoying what they called "The Happy Time." German U-boat crews docked at Lorient to refuel, load fresh torpedoes—and forget with wine and laughter. During "The Happy Time," they tried to forget the destroyers whose depth bombs cracked open submarine hulls like eggshells, drowning crews under tons of ocean.

The Three Aces were U-100 captain Joachim Schepke, U-47 captain Gunther Prien, and U-99 captain Silent Otto Kretschmer. They had sunk more ships than most of the other U-boat commanders combined.

"We are all close to sinking 300,000 tons," the blond Schepke said. "The first to sink his 300,000th ton must be feted with champagne by the others when next we meet at 'The Happy Time.' "

Two days later, Prien's U-47 slid out of port and into the English Channel, followed within hours by Schepke's U-100 and Kretschmer's U-99. For the first time, the Three Aces prowled under the Atlantic at the same time.

MARCH 6: *Washington, the U.S. Senate*

A fter three weeks of debate, the Senate passed the Lend-Lease bill by a resounding vote of 60 to 32. The bill went to the House of Representatives.

MARCH 6: *The Atlantic, near Iceland*

G unther Prien's U-47 saw the smoke of a convoy. He flashed radio signals that drew three other U-boats. The wolfpack chased the convoy and caught up with the ships during a squall.

The British destroyer HMS *Wolverine*'s Asdic system detected the sounds of U-47's propellers. Just before midnight, a *Wolverine* sailor saw the thin, luminous wake of a periscope. *Wolverine* dropped depth bombs. The ocean heaved upward and the U-47 bobbed to the surface.

"Ram!" shouted Commander Jim Rowland on the bridge of *Wolverine*.

Wolverine's steel prow knifed into U-47's hull. Three crewmen scrambled up the hatch and dived free as the U-47 filled with tons of rushing water and took Prien and his crew to their graves on the frigid ocean floor.

MARCH 7, NEAR MIDNIGHT: *10,000 feet above the English Channel*

The Heinkel's pilot saw a dot of light suddenly appear on the left side of his windshield. "That's London forty miles away," said his navigator.

The bomber droned toward London. The dot of light widened until it covered the entire windshield. The bomber descended toward London. At 5,000 feet, the flames of burning London filled the Heinkel's cabin with a light as dazzling as the noon sun.

MARCH 7, NEAR MIDNIGHT: *London, Café de Paris*

Hundreds of women and uniformed sailors and soldiers danced the fox-trot as "Snake Hips" Johnson's swing band played that new American hit, "I'll Never Smile Again." The air-raid sirens wailed outside. But it was Saturday night, and who wanted to sit out a Saturday night in a foul-smelling air-raid shelter? The band began the newest American hit, "Oh, Johnny!" Dancers squeezed onto the floor.

When the bomb hit the roof, debris showered down on the dancers. Screams pierced the roar of crashing plaster and brick. A wall col-

London aflame after a German bombing. The incendiary bombs landed on rooftops and immediately set them on fire. The white-hot bombs burned their way downward through the buildings, setting each floor ablaze. Firefighters wore asbestos suits as they walked into buildings like this one trying to put out the flames. *(National Archives)*

lapsed, burying the bandleader and more than two dozen dancers.

Blood streamed across the floor and swirled around high-heeled shoes and pretty dresses, torn jackets and broken glass.

Medics climbed over smashed girders, their flashlights probing the smoky blackness as they searched for the screaming injured.

Dazed survivors climbed broken stairs to the street. Flames four stories high forced them back. Bombs had cracked open hundreds of the 30,000 miles of gas pipes under London streets. Tongues of gas-fed fire leaped upward into the blackness.

The all-clear sounded. The Café de Paris survivors wandered into another club. A Canadian soldier asked the bandleader to play "Oh, Johnny." "It was the last dance for a friend of mine," the soldier said.

MARCH 8: *Amsterdam, German-occupied Netherlands*

The twenty Dutch men filed into the courtroom to face the military judge. He ordered that ten should be shot for sabotage against the German army. He sentenced the other ten to concentration camps. The judge said that a growing underground army of men and women sneaked out at night to shoot and stab German soldiers, hurling the bodies into canals.

"Resistance fighters will be shot," the judge thundered. "To even think against us is dangerous."

MARCH 10: *Washington, the War Department*

The Army announced that draftees and volunteers had increased the Army to more than a million men. The Navy had increased to 227,000 officers and men and about 50,000 Marines. "If Britain falls," said Secretary of the Navy Frank Knox, "her navy will go to the bottom. Germany, Japan, and Italy will outnumber our ships two to one."

MARCH 11: *Washington, the Oval Office*

The President signed the Lend-Lease bill to make it law only sixty minutes after it passed the House of Representatives. He told Congress that more than $7 billion—almost half of the $17 billion the U.S. would spend this year—would buy ships, guns, planes, and tanks for England and Greece.

MARCH 12: *Salonika, Greece*

The first troops of General Wavell's Army of the Nile landed here, sixty miles from where German troops were lined up along the Greek-Bulgarian frontier. Most of the Nile Army troops were from New Zealand and Australia.

MARCH 16: *Berlin, the Zeughaus*

Speaking to sixty field marshals in the war museum on Germany's Decoration Day, Hitler roared, his right arm flailing the air: "No power, no support coming from any place in the world, can change the outcome of this battle. England will fall!"

MARCH 17: *The Atlantic, off Scotland*

On the bridge of the British destroyer HMS *Walker,* Captain Donald Macintyre turned toward the explosion that shattered the midnight silence of the sea. He saw a white ball of light that blinded him. A submarine's torpedo had just blown up the *Erdosa,* a 10,000-ton oil tanker. The blast incinerated the forty-man crew. Macintyre stared, "shocked into silence," he said later, "by the horror of it."

The surviving German Aces, Otto Kretschmer in U-99 and Joachim Schepke in U-100, had joined a wolfpack to shadow Macintyre's convoy HX 122. Their first victim now burned in front of Macintyre's eyes.

MARCH 17: *Below the Atlantic, off Scotland*

As darkness fell, Kretschmer hung his U-99 between two columns of ships in the convoy. Lining up one ship after another in the sights of his periscope, he launched torpedoes that exploded and sank six flaming ships.

Pacing his bridge, a frantic Captain Macintyre said later, "I racked my brains to find some way to stop the holocaust." His *Asdic* could not locate the subs.

Another destroyer, *Vanoc,* had a new antisubmarine device that sent radio signals underwater. When the signals hit a sub, they bounced back to show the sub on a screen. *Vanoc* signaled that it had located a sub.

The destroyers criss-crossed the area, dropping depth charges. The explosions shook Schepke's U-100, throwing men against the walls, shattering lights. One last explosion heaved U-100 to the surface.

A lone German survivor shouts for help to the British sailors who dropped the depth bombs that destroyed his U-boat. As radar became more effective in spotting U-boats, the German crews begin to say that they traveled under "a glass sea" through which destroyers could see them. *(National Archives)*

Vanoc's captain saw the U-100 trying to slip away in the blackness. "Stand by to ram!" an officer shouted.

Vanoc churned toward the crawling sub. "She'll miss us astern!" Schepke shouted, looking through the periscope. But *Vanoc* clipped U-100's hull. The broken periscope shaft pinned Schepke against the hull. U-100 crewmen dived into the water, but Schepke and fifty other crewmen were dragged down with the broken-backed U-100. Radar—*Vanoc*'s secret device—had scored its first victory at sea.

Walker's Asdic operator picked up sounds from another sub—Kretschmer's U-99. The depth charges had cracked U-99's hull. Its crew stood with water rising to their waists. Sailors clambered to the submarine's deck and dived into the icy water, swimming to the *Walker*. Kretschmer dived off last. He came aboard the *Walker* and stiffly saluted Macintyre. The last of the Three Aces still lived—but as a prisoner of war.

The next morning, Macintyre invited Kretschmer to the bridge. Silent Otto stood grim-faced as he gazed out at the convoy, the ships stretching from horizon to horizon and steaming toward England.

MARCH 23: *Los Angeles, an army induction center*

The gangling, twenty-six-year-old Jimmy Stewart stood in a line with twenty-five other men and raised his right hand. He swore "to bear true faith and allegiance to the United States of America." Photographers' flashbulbs lit his face as Stewart switched jobs. He had been a $12,000-a-month movie star. Now he was a $21-a-month soldier.

Private Stewart boarded a bus that took him and two dozen other new soldiers to nearby Fort MacArthur. "You guys make up Roster Number Five, Company B," a sergeant told them. "Tomorrow morning at six, when I yell Roster Five, you guys tumble out!"

All of the Roster Five soldiers were white. Black draftees and volunteers were assigned to

Movie star Jimmy Stewart goes over some final papers before reporting to the Army. He had won an Oscar in 1940 for his role in *The Philadelphia Story.* After basic training, Private Jimmy Stewart went to Officers Candidate School and won his gold bars as a Second Lieutenant in the Air Corps. *(From the author's collection)*

what the Army called "all-colored" or "all-Negro" units. Black soldiers lived in all-black barracks. Most would serve in all-black units, many in service units as truck drivers and cooks. Black sailors were trained to serve food to officers. In an America where schools, hotels, and restaurants—both in the North and South—were often segregated, the United States' Army and Navy kept whites in all-white barracks and blacks in all-black barracks.

MARCH 27: *Belgrade, Yugoslavia*

Mobs of smiling men, women, and teenagers raced through the streets of the capital, shouting to Americans, "We are with you and England!" They swore to American reporters that Hitler would not march his troops through Yugoslavia to attack Greece.

Two days earlier, the Yugoslavian prime minister had signed the Tripartite Pact, joining the Axis. But this morning, army troops had arrested the government's leaders. Army generals placed a king's crown on the head of the seventeen-year-old Prince Peter. The new king said that his government would not join the Axis. The generals ordered a million and a half troops to the border to stop a German invasion.

MARCH 27: *Berlin, the Reich Chancellory*

Hitler angrily shook the telegram he had just received telling him of the revolution in Yugoslavia. "I have decided to destroy Yugoslavia," he shouted at General Halder. "How much military force do you need, how much time?"

Halder stared, aghast. To attack Yugoslavia, he told Hitler, "We will have to postpone by four weeks the attack on Russia." Halder had ordered only summer uniforms for the troops attacking Russia. He and Hitler believed that the German army would roll over the poorly trained Red Army troops long before winter struck.

Halder and other German generals argued with Hitler. Ignore Yugoslavia for now, the generals told Hitler. We can smash Greece before the Yugoslavians can come to the aid of the Greeks. Then Germany could begin the invasion of Russia early in May, six months before winter.

Hitler would not listen. The Yugoslavs had betrayed him; they must be punished. "The blow against Yugoslavia," he shouted, eyes aglow, "will be carried out with merciless harshness, and the military destruction will be done in blitzkrieg style. . . . It is time to . . . teach the people of Yugoslavia a good lesson."

MARCH 31: *Marsa el Brega, Libya*

General Rommel's fifty tanks rumbled forward, spread wide so the British Tommies would think they faced a three-mile-wide charge. "Panzers to the head of all formations!" Rommel told his tank drivers. "Rear vehicles to raise dust—nothing but dust!" All that dust, he hoped, would fool the British into thinking that the tank charge was three miles deep.

British infantryman were fooled by the trick, and Rommel's troops now called him the Desert Fox. "Mass retreat!" shouted one frightened British soldier. "The Jerries are coming!"

White-faced British soldiers jammed into trucks and rode away from that roaring dust storm. The trucks sped toward the escape port of Tobruk 800 miles away, an eight-day flight from the Desert Fox that a British general called "the most inglorious days in the history of the British army."

Chapter Four

APRIL 1: *Berlin, Army Staff Headquarters*

General Halder dictated the new orders to the captain, who typed them on a paper marked "Secret." The invasions of Greece and Yugoslavia would begin on April 6. But the invasion of Russia, scheduled for May 15, had to be postponed until Greece and Yugoslavia fell. Then two million troops would be shunted back to Poland to smash into Russia on June 22—the new date for Operation Barbarossa.

Halder hoped Russia could be conquered in six weeks—before summer ended. Hitler had ordered the troops to invade Russia carrying only summer uniforms. Hitler was sure Russia could be conquered in a few months. "Kick in the door," he told his generals, "and the whole rotten building will fall down."

APRIL 2: *Washington, the Oval Office*

"Mr. President," said the red-haired, freckle-faced Walter Reuther, "there are automobile plants in Detroit that are running at half speed because the companies built more cars than they can sell. There are thousands of skilled workers who are out of work. Put those men and those factories to work and we can turn out five hundred fighter planes a day."

Roosevelt told Reuther, a Detroit union leader, to talk to the towering, six-foot-three Bill Knudsen and the wiry, chain-smoking Sidney Hillman. Knudsen had been a business executive, Hillman a labor leader. Roosevelt had asked the two men to spur American businessmen and workers into turning out more weapons for England's war and America's defense.

"Walter's right," FDR told Knudsen and Hillman, waving his long cigarette holder. How could they turn those auto plants into factories making tanks and planes?

Bill Knudsen was already telling factory owners: "Turn out all the defense stuff that you can as fast as you can. We'll pay your costs, plus you'll get a fair profit."

Hillman told workers: "You'll get top pay in defense factories, but there can be no strikes that slow down assembly lines."

As automobile plants began to turn out tanks and planes instead of cars and refrigerators, women took jobs formerly held by men. The men were gone to the Army or Navy. Women named Barbara and Mary and Rosie were hammering rivets to build planes, tanks, and ships.

Women workers stitch together the fuselage of a bomber at a defense plant. Women were being hired because men were being drafted into the army. These women workers had a fictional heroine, named Rosie the Riveter, who became a symbol of housewives and other women joining the effort to defend America. *(National Archives)*

APRIL 2: *Berlin, the Reich Chancellory*

Hitler and Japan's foreign minister, Yosuke Matsuoka, bowed formally to each other and sat down. Matsuoka had come to Europe to talk with the Axis dictators, Hitler and Mussolini, and to Russia's dictator, Josef Stalin.

Hitler knew what Japan wanted—the colonies of Southeast Asia, from India to Singapore, that were owned by Holland, France, and England. He knew that the U.S.-owned Philippine Islands blocked Japan's road to Southeast Asia.

England would soon fall, Hitler assured Matsuoka. America would then stand alone against Germany, Italy, and Japan.

"Therefore," said Hitler in his most sugary way, "never in the human imagination" was there a better time than now for Japan to strike southward. "Such a moment," he said, "would never return."

And if America should try to stop Japan, Hitler promised the Japanese foreign minister, "Germany would promptly take part in case of a conflict between Japan and America.' Japan could count on Hitler's blitzkrieging army to defeat America.

APRIL 5: *Hollywood*

Men in army khaki and navy blue now filled the streets of cities across the nation. Film studios began to make movies about soldiers and sailors. Audiences roared with laughter at *Buck Privates,* starring comedians Bud Abbott and Lou Costello as a pair of bumbling soldiers. In that movie the three Andrews Sisters sang a song that became a hit: "Boogie Woogie Bugle Boy from Company B."

APRIL 6: *Belgrade, Yugoslavia*

The bells of Palm Sunday had just begun to peal when the first wave of German bombers—Heinkels, Dorniers, and Stukas—droned above the city. People stuck their heads out windows, rubbing sleep from their eyes. They saw the Stukas dive. Black sticks plummeted earthward.

Streets heaved upward. Buildings vanished in eruptions of black smoke. "It was like the crack of a hundred-yard whip," one stunned

Sailors in Navy blue and soldiers in Army khaki had become familiar sights on the streets of America. The servicemen came home on weekend leaves to go to places of entertainment, like this amusement park, for a night of fun. *(Library of Congress)*

man said. In her bedroom a fourteen-year-old girl had put a new silver slipper on her right foot. A bomb's shock waves and flying slivers of metal threw her against the wall. She looked down at the reddening floor and saw that the slipper was gone and so was her left leg.

For seventy-two hours the Luftwaffe rained bombs onto the defenseless people who had dared to say "no" to Hilter. Tongues of fire leaped over 10,000 shattered buildings and 17,000 dead. Belgrade had felt the lash of Hitler's Operation Punishment.

APRIL 6: *The Yugoslavian-Greek borders*

The German 12th Army rolled into Yugoslavia. More than two million German, Rumanian, and Bulgarian troops plunged into Greece, cutting off the Greek Army of the Piraeus fighting the Italians in Albania.

APRIL 8: *Koziani Pass near Larissa, Greece*

The Australian machine gunner crouched over his weapon overlooking the winding road through the pass. He had come to Greece from North Africa with the British Expeditionary Force—about 50,000 troops, mostly Australians and New Zealanders. The Greeks and the BEF, he told a *New York Times* war correspondent, were being overwhelmed by masses of Bulgarian, Rumanian, and German suicide squads who hurled themselves at his gun's spitting bullets.

"They came up the side of the road like flies," he said, his face pale and coated with dirt. He had not slept in twenty-four hours. "We were giving it to them on all sides, and they went down like you see in the movies. It was just like a movie. I would not have believed it."

APRIL 10: *Rome, Via Venetia*

Crowds massed in the thoroughfare after Rome Radio announced that German troops had captured the Greek stronghold at Salonika. The Greek Army of the Iparus was cut off in Albania, where it had shoved back Italian armies. Thousands of Greeks were surrendering.

"We feel we have come out of a nightmare," an Italian soldier, wounded in Albania, told an American reporter. "Our goose was cooked until the Germans came to save us."

APRIL 13: *Belgrade, Yugoslavia*

German troops rode through the broken glass and rubble on the city's main avenue. They stared with awe at the still-smoking ruins, seeing orphaned and homeless children, their clothes tattered, begging for food.

APR. 13: *Cairo, headquarters of the Army of the Nile*

General Wavell stared at the map. General Rommel's patrols had crossed the Libyan border into Egypt. In two weeks, the German tanks had rumbled to within 200 miles of Cairo and the Suez Canal.

"Defend Tobruk to the death!" Churchill had cabled Wavell—and Wavell knew why. Rommel needed fresh water to supply his Afrika Korps driving across the desert to Cairo. Rommel could get that water only from tankers docking at Tobruk. Rommel had to take the port to continue his drive toward Cairo.

But the bulk of Wavell's Army of the Nile had gone to Greece. "If Rommel takes Tobruk," Wavell told his commanders, "there is nothing between the Germans and Cairo."

APRIL 16: *Tobruk, Libya*

The parched and dusty British and Anzac (Australian and New Zealand) troops clambered down from the trucks that had carried them half a step ahead of Rommel's tanks. Crouched in dugouts and behind sandbags, they watched the cannons of the huge Mark IVs aimed straight at them. For the Rats of Tobruk—as they called themselves—the siege had begun for the port that Rommel had to win.

APRIL 16: *Kiafe Lusit Pass, northern Greece*

Corporal Mikia Pezas cowered in the deep trench with three other soldiers and their captain. They gripped their saucerlike helmets as Italian shells blew geysers of dirt all around them.

"Who will go to the OP [Observation Post]

and bring back a message to tell me what's going on?" shouted the captain between bomb bursts.

Mouth dry, Mikia surprised himself by standing up to volunteer. Corporal Yannacopoulos also volunteered. "I'll go first," Yannacopoulos shouted to Mikia above the roar of the bombardment.

The corporal weaved between craters toward the OP about 800 yards away. Mikia dashed after him, twisting behind boulders as shards of steel whistled around him. Mikia dived to safety behind a huge boulder. His heart pounded so fiercely that he feared his chest might burst. He told himself that he could go no farther.

"I'll go back," he told himself. But then he thought: "What will the captain say?"

He jerked his lucky omen, a bat's bone, from his tunic. Gripping the bone, he crawled forward, his face in the dirt. Suddenly the earth stopped shaking and the bombardment ended. He looked up and saw Yannacopoulos stretched behind a boulder.

"Come on, Yannacopoulos," Mikia shouted. "It's quiet now."

Yannacopoulos did not move. Mikia ran to his side and looked down into a face that was a pool of blood.

Mikia dashed to the OP and got a message for his captain. Back in the trench, he remembered what Yannacopolous had told him a few days ago: "March is the bloodiest month." March had stayed late for the twenty-eight-year-old father of four.

APRIL 22: *Berlin, Ministry of Information*

T he German officer stood before the assembled war correspondents. In a barking voice he said, "The new Yugoslavian government has announced its unconditional surrender to the armies of the Tripartite Pact."

APRIL 23: *Rome, Piazza Venezia*

"*Viva Mussolini! Viva Mussolini!*" Crowds roared for Il Duce to appear on the balcony. Men and women waved bottles of champagne to celebrate the news that Rome Radio had just announced: "The unconditional surrender of the 250,000-man Greek army."

APRIL 26: *Athens, the Acropolis*

G erman tanks wheeled by the ancient ruins. Minutes later, the swastika floated over the capital. German planes roared toward the nearby Greek ports to strafe and bomb the British as the BEF boarded ships to ferry the troops back to Egypt. Of the 50,000 troops who had landed in Greece, about 10,000 had been killed, wounded, or captured.

APRIL 26: *With BEF troops aboard the SS* Julia, *bound for Cairo*

A medical officer, Captain Theodore Stephanides, crouched on the deck watching the Stuka peel away from the formation of bombers. It dived, its hyenalike screech growing louder in the captain's ears. The Stuka swooped over the smokestack and a black speck tumbled from its belly. Moments later, the ship lurched and pitched as water fountained higher than the masts. The bomb that could have blown the *Julia* to bits had missed by only twenty yards.

The *Julia* lumbered on toward Egypt, its hull cracked and leaking. "Another bloody Dunkirk," a sergeant growled.

APRIL 26: *Boston, Harvard Square*

A placard posted by Harvard students listed the fifteen nations conquered by Hitler in less than three years. They were Austria and the French Sudetenland in 1938; Czechoslovakia and Poland in 1939; Denmark, Norway, Luxembourg, the Netherlands, Belgium, France, Hungary, and Rumania in 1940; Bulgaria, Yugoslavia, and Greece in 1941. In 1938, Hitler had ruled over about 180,000 square miles of territory and 79 million Germans; in May of 1941, he towered over more than 760,000 square miles and dictated to more than 150 million Europeans.

APRIL 26: *Moscow, the Kremlin*

The burly, mustached Josef Stalin stood, smiling as the German ambassador to Russia, Count Frederick von der Schulenburg, came into the room. Stalin threw a heavy arm around Schulenburg's shoulder. "We must remain friends, you and I," Stalin said. "And you must do everything when you go to Berlin to keep us good friends."

Count von Schulenburg was flying to Berlin the next day for a meeting with Hitler. Stalin wanted the count to speak well of him to Hitler.

Stalin had been brooding because Hitler had not replied to his messages for the past few months. He suspected that Hitler might attack Russia in a year or two. In his book about himself, *Mein Kampf,* Hitler had written that he wanted German farmers raising crops on Russian farmlands.

Stalin hoped to hold off an attack until 1942 while he built up his army and air force. During the 1930s he had weakened his army, shooting his top generals. He had feared the army might seize control and take the government away from his Communist Party. But now he needed smart generals and a strong army to defend Russia against an enemy he had come to dread.

To hold off an attack by Hitler, Stalin had sold to Hitler—at cheap prices—the grain, iron, coal, and other fuels that Hitler needed. Now Stalin decided to be even more generous.

"Tell my dear Adolf," Stalin told the ambassador, "that we will soon be sending to his hungry armies more than five million tons of Russian grain."

APRIL 28: *Berlin, the Reich Chancellory*

Count von Schulenburg told Hitler of Stalin's gift of wheat. Hitler stared back at the ambassador, his face as hard as stone. He did not tell von Schulenburg that his armies were gathering to plunge into "that rotten building."

Russia was filled with two kinds of people Hitler had sworn for twenty years to destroy: Communists and Jews.

That hatred traced back to his days as a soldier in World War I. As a corporal, Hitler had fought bravely in the front lines. He had been shocked when Germany surrendered to the Allied armies of America, Great Britain, and France.

He blamed Communists and Jews for Germany's defeat. Near the end of the war, the Communist Bolshevik Party had led a mutiny among sailors in the German navy. They had "stabbed Germany in the back," Hitler wrote in *Mein Kampf.* And the stabbers, he had told cheering mobs, were the Communists and the Jews. An insane hatred against Jews and Communists boiled and bubbled in his mind. He vowed to erase from the earth the "vermin Jews and Communists."

When von Schulenburg left, Hitler called in General Halder. He told Halder to summon the General Staff for a meeting. At that meeting he ordered a program of terror that he had kept in the recesses of his mind. It was a program of terror, he told the generals, that would not spare even the most pitiful of the old, or the gentlest of women, or the smallest child, or the newest-born baby.

Chapter Five

MAY 1: *Tobruk, Libya*

Field Marshal Rommel paced furiously in front of his officers. They stood in a tent as artillery roared shells above them. For two days and two nights, the guns of the Afrika Korps had blown holes through the line of Anzacs defending the port that Rommel must win to capture Cairo and the Suez Canal. But when German and Italian troops charged through the holes, machine-gun fire cut them down.

Rommel cursed at his officers for not pushing their troops through those holes. He snapped at an Italian colonel: "I shall expect the immediate execution by the firing squad of officers who show cowardice in the face of the enemy."

A German sergeant crouched low as tracer bullets whizzed over his trench. The sergeant had fought in Poland and France. "But that," he told another Afrika Korps soldier, "was a breeze in the park compared to this."

Some 300 yards away, Australian private Noel Sankey clutched his helmet as he heard the shriek of an incoming shell. He dug his nose deeper into the desert sand. The ground rose up, bouncing him into the air. He landed in a four-foot-deep crater that had not been there moments before. The bomb's smoke choked his lungs—but he thanked God he was still alive.

Two Germans jumped into the crater. They had been trying to creep back to their lines. They stared at Sankey, who stared back. There was no room in the cramped crater for anyone to lift a rifle and fire. An Australian private leaped into the crater, landing atop the two Germans.

An explosion shook the crater. Desert sand rained down on the four soldiers. "You're our prisoners," said one of the Germans. "No," growled Sankey, "you're our prisoners."

Moments later, a third Australian dived into the crater. "We outnumber you," shouted Sankey "you're our prisoners."

The Germans nod-ded. Minutes later, the five slithered out of the crater and crawled to a British outpost.

MAY 4: *Berlin General Staff Headquarters*

G eneral Halder just stared at the tele-gram, his face harden-

An Afrika Korps soldier drinks from his water canteen atop his tank. Both sides wore shorts during the desert warfare, because temperatures during the day could soar to 120 degrees in the shade. *(National Archives)*

ing. Two days of fighting at Tobruk had killed or wounded 1,200 of Rommel's Afrika Korps. "This is a soldier gone stark mad," Halder muttered. He ordered Rommel to encircle Tobruk and try to starve the defenders into surrendering.

The glum Rommel obeyed. But the Desert Fox promised himself to avenge this defeat— the first in World War II by any German corps.

MAY 5: *Berkeley, California*

Professor Peter Pringshelm arrived from Europe to join the physics department at the University of California. A Belgian scientist, he had been among 5,000 Jews rounded up in Antwerp and shipped to a German concentration camp in France. A friend, an American scientist, had written to German friends and the professor had been allowed to leave for America.

Two years earlier, other Jewish scientists had fled Hitler's persecution and arrived in America. They told German-born Albert Einstein that Hitler's scientists were trying to split the atom. A world-famous physicist, Einstein knew what that meant. He wrote to President Roosevelt. Splitting the atom, he wrote, could create a bomb so powerful that "if exploded in a port, [it] might very well destroy the whole port with towns of the surrounding territory."

Roosevelt handed the letter to his military adviser, saying, "This requires action." The Army began secret research on what would be known as the Manhattan Project.

MAY 11: *5,000 feet above Wilhelmshaven, Germany*

Bunny Benson, the Blenheim's bombardier, spoke on the intercom to the bomber's pilot as he stared down the bomb sight. Icicles hung from Bunny's short beard. During the five-hour flight from England to this naval base, the plane had flown at 10,000 feet. The fifty-degree-below-zero air had iced the sweat on Bunny's face.

"Left a bit," Bunny ordered, watching the shipyards flow by below him. "Hold it steady above the chop . . ." The chop was antiaircraft shells now bursting around the Blenheim like big black blossoms.

"Steady . . . steady . . ." Coming over the intercom, Bunny's metallic voice struck gunner Mike Henry's nerves as sharply as a dentist's drill.

"Drop the bombs and let's get out of here," Mike muttered as one ugly black puff shook the plane.

"Steady, steady . . ."

Sergeant Pilot Godfrey Warner felt the Blenheim lurch upward, its heavy load of bombs dropped into what he later called "a forest of flames. We just shoveled bombs into the flames."

"Bandit at two o'clock!" Mike Henry screeched into his mike. The Me-110 fighter arrowed straight at the bomber.

Warner swiveled his neck to look into tracer bullets streaking above his left wing.

He banked the Blenheim hard right, then dived. "We'll head out to sea!" he shouted over the radio.

The Blenheim sped low over the whitecaps of the North Sea. Henry looked back. The bandit had lost them. From twenty miles away, Henry could still see the flames leaping high over the naval shipyards into the midnight-black sky.

MAY 13: *Berlin, Unter den Linden*

Crowds gathered to stare at the smoking ruins of the Bellevue, a mansion where foreign guests stayed while visiting Hitler. Two nights earlier, the heaviest British air raid of the war had blown out the windows of the Berlin Opera House and shaken Hitler's Reich Chancellory. Berliners had to huddle at least once a week in air-raid shelters.

During a raid the night before, a German diplomat sat in a shelter with a Russian visitor and told him, "As I have been telling you, England is defeated."

"I see," said the Russian. "But then tell me, whose bombs are those dropping outside?"

MAY 20: *Tobruk, Libya*

The Sahara Desert's glaring sun drove the noonday temperature to 130 degrees. Fingers blistered when they touched a rifle's barrel. Sudden sandstorms whipped faces so badly that they often bled. The defenders of Tobruk stretched under tin shelters to shield themselves from flying shrapnel, but the sunbaked shelters were oven-hot. The Rats of Tobruk could not move an inch out of those shelters from dawn to dusk. The Germans sprayed anything moving with streams of bullets. The Rats sipped hot, rusty water from their canteens and dreamed of icy Australian streams.

When darkness came, the Rats could move around. They ate breakfast at nine at night, lunch after midnight, supper at five in the morning just before dawn's rising red sun baked them for another day.

At night and at day, the desert was filled by the crumping sounds of mortar fire, the staccato chatter of machine guns and rifles. But precisely at 9:57 each night, silence suddenly fell over the battlefield. Hands turned knobs of radios to a European station where German singer Lale Anderson sang in German and in English a song of men and women separated by war and aching to be together.

"Underneath the lantern
By the barracks gate
Darling I remember
The way you used to wait
'Twas there that you whispered tenderly
That you loved me, that you'd always be
My Lili of the lamplight
My own Lili Marlene."

This Polish soldier was one of the Rats of Tobruk. He and his comrades had escaped to England by sea, after the collapse of Poland. Also fighting in the desert with the British were units of the Free French Army, soldiers who had crossed the Channel to England after the defeat of France. The leader of the Free French government, based in London, was General Charles de Gaulle. *(National Archives)*

MAY 24: *Aboard HMS* Hood *in the North Atlantic*

Just before dawn, Vice Admiral Lancelot Holland saw what British battleships and cruisers had been seeking all week, the *Bismarck,* a fast and huge battleship and the pride of Hitler's navy, which now loomed large on the eastern horizon.

The Germans had sent the *Bismarck* and a big cruiser, the *Prinz Eugen,* into the Atlantic to blow apart convoys of cargo ships and their cruisers and destroyers. A pack of British warships had spotted the two German giants on radar and tracked them for a week.

"Fire!" commanded the *Hood*'s Admiral Holland. The cruiser's gunners winged shells weighing a ton apiece at 1,600 miles an hour across twelve miles of water. Sailors on the *Hood* bridge winced and held their ears at the sound of the guns' roar.

At that moment, the *Prinz Eugen* gunners had zeroed in on the *Hood.* Two of the *Eugen*'s shells hit the *Hood* dead amidship. Hunks of turrets, metal plate, and flesh and bone twirled high into the morning sky.

On the bridge, signalman Edward Briggs looked down at the ocean rushing up toward him as the huge *Hood* keeled to the port side. He dived into the water — water that had been three stories below him seconds ago. When he bobbed to the surface, he saw the bottom of the *Hood* vanish. Of almost 1,500 men on the *Hood,* he was one of only three survivors.

MAY 24: *Aboard HMS* Prince of Wales

Shells from the *Bismarck* and *Prinz Eugen* crashed into the battleship's bridge. Sub-lieutenant Michael Martin rushed up from below deck to see "no bridge—nothing but hairs on it, like dog hairs, and blood—all one's friends." The *Wales* limped out of range of the German guns.

MAY 24: *Aboard the* Bismarck

Admiral Gunther Lutjens knew his ship had been struck below water by shells from the *Prince of Wales.* Holes had been torn in fuel tanks, slowing the ship from more than thirty knots to less than twenty-five. Lutjens turned the *Bismarck* toward France almost a thousand miles away as twenty British warships followed his trail of leaking oil.

MAY 26: *Aboard the* Bismarck, *690 miles west of France*

Lutjens needed only a few more hours to slide under the umbrella of Luftwaffe bombers flying from France to shield him. But HMS *Victory* had sent bombers that exploded torpedoes into the *Bismarck*'s side. Now the giant ship wallowed helplessly in the tossing sea.

Lutjens sent a last signal to Berlin: "We fight to the last shell. Long live the Führer."

The *Bismarck* never fired that last shell. A pack of British warships poured shells on a ship whose guns had been silenced by the bombardment. HMS *Dorsetshire* rammed three torpedoes into the *Bismarck* and she began to keel. Hundreds of German sailors were thrown into the raging, icy ocean. Hundreds of others scurried down the tilting hull.

MAY 27: *Aboard HMS* Dorsetshire

"They look like giant black ants," a sailor said, watching the hundreds of Germans crawling down the angled hull of the *Bismarck*. Moments later, the *Bismarck* vanished in white, foaming water.

British destroyers raced to pick up survivors. They pulled in fewer than a hundred of the shaking, near-frozen Germans. More than a thousand of the *Bismarck* crew thrashed in the frigid water when orders rang out on the bridges of the British ships: "Submarine alert! Full speed!" The British ships sped away, hundred of German bodies mangled by the twisting screws of propellors. Others grasped frantically at hulls flashing by their fingers. More than 2,300 of the *Bismarck* crew, including Lutjens, were left behind to drown.

Chapter Six

JUNE 5: *On an army plane near Fort Benning, Georgia*

The apple-cheeked young soldier stared down from the plane's cargo door at ground whizzing by a thousand feet below. He hooked a line from the parachute on his back to a cable strung inside the plane. A sergeant stood next to him.

"We'll drop to seven hundred and fifty feet," the sergeant told the rookie one last time. "From that height, you'd hit the ground without a chute in eight and a half seconds. When you jump, count to four. Your main chute should open. If it doesn't open, pull the cord on the emergency chute at your chest. It should open in two seconds. That's six seconds gone by, but you'll land OK."

The pale-faced rookie stepped out of the plane. The chute blossomed open. The rookie hit the ground safely. He became the 521st soldier to become an American paratrooper. The year before, the Army had only forty-eight paratroopers. But by this fall, there would be more than 4,000.

JUNE 7: *Chequers, near London, the country home of the Prime Minister*

The portly Churchill sat in his favorite leather chair as he read the latest messages from Hitler to his generals. The messages had been intercepted by Ultra, the British code-breaking machine. Reading the messages, Churchill knew that Hitler planned to invade Russia on June 22.

Churchill began to write a secret message to Sir Stafford Cripps, his ambassador in Moscow. Churchill told Cripps to warn Stalin that Hitler was planning to attack him on June 22.

JUNE 13: *Tokyo, German News Bureau*

German correspondent Richard Sorge liked to imagine himself as the dashing, trench-coated reporter who entranced women. But now he wondered what he was doing wrong.

Two weeks earlier a German army officer, stationed in Tokyo, had given Sorge a news tip: Hitler would invade Russia on June 22. The officer had no way of knowing that Sorge was a Russian spy.

Sorge had sent a coded message to his spy chiefs in Moscow, giving them the date for the invasion. But after two weeks, not a word had come back to him from Moscow. Sorge decided to send a coded message directly to Stalin warning him that Germany would invade Russia on June 22.

JUNE 14: *Berlin, the Reich Chancellory*

Hitler strode into the Cabinet Room and 200 generals snapped to attention. Two years earlier, the generals had sneered at Hitler—behind his back—as "that World War I corporal." But his lightning victories from France to Greece had stunned then. Now they looked at him with awe.

Hitler strode to a podium, his eyes glaring as he motioned his cowed generals to be seated.

In an earlier order, he had informed the generals that Barbarossa would do more than throw open the vastness of Russia to the German people. His army and black-clad SS troopers, he had told them, would "liquidate the Communist system." He had reminded the generals what he had written in his autobiography, *Mein Kampf:* ". . . the end of the Jewish domination in Russia will also be the end of Russia as a state."

On this day, Hitler spoke from eleven in the morning until six at night. He told the generals that all persons "accused of crimes against the German invaders should be brought to officers and shot immediately." And he added that Jews as well as Communist Party leaders—called commissars—were criminals. "It is not our job," he told his generals, "to see that these criminals survive."

He knew that the generals believed it was a war crime to kill prisoners of war. "All officers," he growled, "will have to rid themselves" of such old-fashioned ideas. "I insist absolutely that my orders be executed. . . ."

The generals sat mute as mice.

JUNE 15: *Moscow, the Kremlin*

Josef Stalin sat at a table facing two of his chief commanders. Marshal Rodion Malinovsky seemed to have a flagpole for a spine. The other was the balding, burly Marshal Semin Timoshenko. The Russian dictator had just showed them the messages from Cripps and Sorge, both warning of an invasion of Russia on June 22.

"The messages are tricks born in the mind of Churchill," Stalin said. He knew that Cripps obeyed Churchill's orders. And Sorge, he thought, was probably a double agent, also working for the British. Stalin knew that Churchill wanted Russia's millions to join him in the war against Hitler. Churchill had his back to the wall, Stalin said, and wanted all the help he could get.

Stalin dreaded a war with Hitler. He feared Hitler's blitzkrieg would steamroll across Russia. He knew he needed at least a year of rebuilding his army in order to stand a chance against Hitler's armored fist.

The two generals told Stalin that Hitler was massing millions of troops along the Russian border for almost a thousand miles.

Stalin smiled. As a youth, he had robbed banks. He knew a robbery when he saw one. Hitler, he said, was trying to scare Russia by stealing more oil and grain at cheaper prices. Hitler, he reminded the commanders, had signed a peace treaty with Russia only a year and a half before.

"But what should we do if we are fired at and attacked?" Timoshenko asked.

"Do not fire back!" Stalin said quickly. "Hitler might use that as an excuse to attack."

JUNE 16–17: *Halfaya Pass, Libya*

The heavyset artillery colonel, Wilhelm Bach, puffed on a cigar as he gripped the long-range binoculars. He could hear the hum of engines growing louder as the British column of tanks advanced toward the pass. General Wavell was launching Operation Battleaxe. It was an attempt to rescue The Rats of Tobruk.

More than 300 new Mark IV tanks rumbled forward to back up Bach's guns. The tanks and fresh troops had just arrived from Greece to reinforce Field Marshal Rommel's growing Afrika Korps.

Rommel's tanks and guns blocked this 300-foot-deep valley. Tommy, as the British troops were called, would have to fight his way through this pass to reach Tobruk and free its defenders.

The roar of the advancing British tanks grew louder. Gripping his binoculars, Bach estimated they were two miles away. He shouted at an officer: "No one fire! Let them come on!"

His artillerymen crouched behind the long barrels of guns never before fired at tanks—giant antiaircraft guns.

Clouds of dust billowed up from the desert as the tanks came within a mile of the German guns. Bach raised his hand. "Fire!" The ack-ack guns belched smoke as they whizzed twenty-two-pound shells at 400 miles an hour.

The shells blew holes in the tanks. Fuel tanks erupted. Tanks vanished in explosions of black smoke and orange flame. "They're tearing the tanks to pieces!" a British colonel radioed Wavell, who flew overhead in a light plane.

The British tanks tried to ram through a pass filled with smoke and the flash and thunder of guns. Tanks battled tanks like prehistoric monsters, blazing fire at point-blank range. The battle's survivors would forever call this place "Hell's Fire Pass."

Wavell stared down from his plane at a trail of blackened, smoking Tiger tanks. The British turned and limped back into Egypt. Wavell cabled Churchill: "I am sorry to tell you of Operation Battleaxe's failure." Rommel still needed only to capture Tobruk—and its water—to roll to the Suez Canal against a shattered Army of the Nile.

JUNE 18: *Tokyo, Imperial Naval Headquarters*

The Japanese navy's chief of the general staff, sixty-two-year-old Admiral Osami Nagano, listened attentively as his officers quizzed Admiral Yamamoto about his plan to attack America's Pacific Fleet at Pearl Harbor. Nagano's cannonball-shaped, balding head glistened in the warm room. The more the supreme commander heard of Yamamoto's plan, the more he thought it crazy.

"How can you sail undetected some five thousand miles from Japan to Pearl Harbor with more than thirty battleships, cruisers, and aircraft carriers, plus their fuel tankers?" a staff officer asked Yamamoto in a sneering way. "You will surely be seen during a voyage of almost three weeks."

"We will go north where the sea is stormy and has little traffic in December," Yamamoto said calmly. "The American planes based at Pearl Harbor can only spot us when we will be about a hundred miles away—too late to stop our carriers from launching their planes."

"But, Admiral," asked another officer, "how can you be sure that the American fleet will be anchored at Pearl Harbor when you will have been at sea for almost a month? When your bombers arrive, there may be no ships to bomb."

"We have ways of knowing," answered Yamamoto with a slight smile, "when the fleet leaves Pearl Harbor and when it comes back to anchor."

JUNE 20: *Honolulu, Hawaii*

The slender Takeo Yoshikawa stepped out of the Japanese Consulate at 1742 Nuuan Street. A yellow, battered taxi stood at the curb. Yoshikawa slid into the back seat. The driver steered the car south on Nuuan Street. The taxi driver was one of thousands of Japanese who had come to Hawaii to work, many as servants for American families.

Yoshikawa scribbled notes in the back seat. His official title was consulate clerk. But the other clerks saw him sit around the office most of the day. They gossiped that he had more important duties than clerking.

The taxi wheezed to a stop on a dock at Pearl City, which overlooked the Pearl Harbor naval base. Peering out from the rear of the taxi, Yoshikawa could see the American battlewagons moored side by side.

That night, Yoshikawa sent a coded message to Tokyo. Admiral Yamamoto read it a few hours later. The message assured the admiral that he would know from day to day when the Pacific fleet entered and left Pearl Harbor.

JUNE 22: *The Russian-Polish border*

First Lieutenant Hermann Zumpke hugged the side of the ditch that stretched near the railroad track. The track ran across a bridge

Hurling the "potato-masher" type of hand grenade, a German soldier is protected by a rifleman as he lifts himself up to throw the explosive at a Russian machine-gun nest. At one place on the border, a German and a Russian sentry met every five minutes during their patrolling. They usually exchanged a few words. But, as the moment arrived for the German attack on Russia, the German sentry came up to the unsuspecting Russian, stabbed him, and rushed across the border. *(National Archives)*

into Russia. He glanced at the luminous dial of his watch: 3:15 A.M.

Seconds later 7,000 German guns thundered, throwing up sheets of stabbing white light along the border for almost a thousand miles.

"Let's go!" Zumpke shouted. He gripped a submachine gun. His infantrymen stood up, their helmets like steel pods in the high grass behind the ditch. Zumpke ran across the railroad bridge. His hobnailed boots clattered on the wooden boards. Zumpke saw a Russian sentry leap from a box at the end of the bridge. The sentry stared, shock on his face, then raised his rifle. Zumpke triggered a burst. The fatally wounded sentry toppled backward, crashing onto the boards. His sightless eyes stared upward as Zumpke and some three million German, Rumanian, Bulgarian, Finnish, and Italian soldiers surged into Russia.

JUNE 22: *Moscow, Red Army Headquarters*

The warm morning breeze fluttered the curtains in the office of Marshal Timoshenko. In one corner, Timoshenko's thin-faced, bespectacled chief of staff, General Georgi Zhukov, hunched behind a desk as he scanned reports from the border. His phone rang. He picked it up, listened, spoke a few orders, and hung up. He turned to an aide and said, "German aircraft are bombing Kovno, Rovno, Sevastapol, and Odessa. We reported that to Stalin, but he told me it was only Hitler's way of trying to provoke us into attacking. . . ." Zhukov threw up his hands in disgust.

At that moment his chief, Marshal Timoshenko, was sending an order to commanders of the 134 Russian divisions—about two million men—facing the Germans. "No actions are to be taken against the Germans without our consent."

JUNE 22: *Bialystok, Western Military District*
Headquarters of the Red Army

General Ivan Boldin scanned dozens of messages that had crossed his desk, reports of German planes, tanks, and infantry swarming over the border. Then he saw the message from Timoshenko. He radioed a message to Timoshenko: "Cities are being bombed, people are dying. . . . We must act . . . the Germans have started a war!"

JUNE 23: *Moscow, the Kremlin*

One of Stalin's young aides, the moon-faced, hulking Nikita Khrushchev, watched the reports clack over a teletype machine. In only half a day of war, more than 1,200 of Russia's 8,000 warplanes had been destroyed on the ground by strafing fighters and bombers. Divisions of 20,000 men had vanished as though run over by a vacuum cleaner. In just a few hours, the German spearhead had plunged one hundred miles into Russia, killing or capturing more than 100,000 bewildered Russians.

Khrushchev watched the teletype spew out frantic requests from army generals at the front: "Should we attack? How should we attack? Where should we attack?"

They got no answers from Generalissimo Stalin. Khrushchev had stood for hours outside the door of a second-story Kremlin room where Josef Stalin was now hiding. Stalin often went to the room to drain bottles of vodka with his drinking partners. When news came that Hitler had struck, Stalin fled into the room. Khrushchev and other aides banged at the door but heard only silence.

JUNE 23: *New York City*

Former president Herbert Hoover, a fervent anti-Communist, told reporters that America should let two evils wipe out each other. "Let Hitler and Stalin kill each other," the cherub-faced Hoover said.

Ever since Nikolai Lenin and his Communist Party had set up the world's first communist state in Russia some twenty years before, Hoover had blasted communism. He still believed that Stalin's Communist dictatorship was just as cruel and bloody-handed as Hitler's Nazism and Mussolini's fascism.

"Roosevelt is reported to be ready to send Lend-Lease aid to Russia," a reporter said.

"The President spoke of the Four Freedoms," Hoover growled. "Where is any freedom in Russia? Aid to Russia in the name of the Four Freedoms is a gargantuan joke."

JUNE 25: *Washington, the Oval Office*

His white-haired secretary, Grace Tully, took down the words as the President dictated a letter to a friend, William Leahy. "I think if I give him [Stalin] everything I can and ask nothing from him in return . . . he won't try to annex any more territory," the President told Leahy.

Leahy had reminded Roosevelt how Stalin had grabbed Lithuania and other hunks of Eastern Europe after Hitler smashed Poland.

Roosevelt brushed aside Leahy's reminder. ". . . I do not think we need worry about any possibility of Russian domination" of Europe, he wrote. Anyway, Roosevelt told Leahy, Russian soldiers who killed millions of Germans could save Americans from going to Europe to die.

JUNE 26: *Moscow, the Kremlin*

Nikita Khrushchev banged once more on the door of the second-story room, begging Stalin to come out and direct his reeling armies. He heard an anguished bawl:

"No! No! All that Lenin created, we have lost!"

Chapter Seven

JULY 1: *The Wolf's Lair, Hitler's Russian-campaign headquarters hidden in a forest in eastern Poland*

Hitler stared at maps spread out on a long table by the army's commander in chief, Marshal Walter von Brauchitsch. Next to von Brauchitsch stood General Halder.

Halder swung a long pointer at the maps. German tanks, he said, were racing toward Moscow at better than fifty miles a day. Only Russia's rutted roads slowed them down.

"The war," Halder told Hitler, "will be over in a matter of weeks."

JULY 2: *Tokyo, the Imperial Palace*

Emperor Hirohito entered the room. The Emperor's generals, admirals, and statesmen bowed deeply to the man the Japanese looked upon as a god. When the Emperor took his seat, this year's Imperial Conference began.

Hideki Tojo, a short and chesty general with a look of arrogance on his mustached face, argued that 1941 should be the year Japan struck southward to seize the Asian colonies owned for centuries by non-Asians. Japan, he said, could give prosperity to Asians whose countries had been plundered by Europeans and Americans. There was no better time than now, he went on, to bring those countries under the tent of Japan's "Greater Co-Prosperity Sphere." France and Holland lay defeated. Great Britain stood only one blow away from falling under the boots of Hitler.

"In carrying out the plans outlined," Tojo read from the Conference's report to the Emperor, "we will not be deterred by the possibility of being involved in war with England and America."

JULY 3: *Tokyo, Foreign Ministry*
The Imperial Conference report was radioed in code to Japanese diplomats around the world.

JULY 3: *Washington, Japanese Embassy*
With his one good eye, Ambassador Nomura read the Conference report and frowned. He had been assuring President Roosevelt that Japan did not want war with the United States.

JULY 3: *Washington, the Navy Department*
Smiles broke out on the faces of Magic's code breakers as they decoded the report sent to Nomura. The sailors and officers were smiling, because Japan had not changed the

code even though someone in Tokyo had suspected that the Americans could read it.

A few hours later, a grim President and his
secretary of state, the silver-haired Cordell
Hull, read the Imperial Conference report. Japan's military hungered to ram south with their
ships, tanks, and planes. Roosevelt and Hull
knew they had the means of making those war
machines chug to a stop. But that might push
Japan toward reaching for the sword.

JULY 12: *Moscow, the Kremlin*

A ir-raid sirens wailed. Stalin and Khrushchev rushed to a window and watched
the bombs drop from the Heinkels. The Kremlin's walls shook as Hitler dropped his first
bombs on Moscow.

Stalin came out of hiding and shook off his
fright. Speaking on radio, he told the Russian
people that Hitler wanted to turn them "into
the slaves of German princes." He begged Russian civilians to "scorch the earth" before leaving their farms and fleeing from the onrushing
Germans. "Leave them nothing to eat—no
grain, no cattle," he exhorted.

JULY 13: *Moscow, Army Headquarters*

T wo Russian generals, P. V. Rychagov and
A. A. Korobkov, arrived as ordered, relieved of their commands of armies in northern
Russia. The Germans had swept over both armies.

A captain told the generals that Stalin had ordered them arrested. "Why?" shouted Rychagov. The captain shrugged and signaled to a sergeant. Minutes later, the two generals faced a firing squad and were shot.

JULY 13: *Moscow, the Kremlin*

S talin studied a sheet showing this month's production of tanks and planes by Russian factories. Stalin had expected war with Hitler — but not until 1942. He had built war factories in small towns scattered over Russia. The factories rolled out planes and tanks at twice the number that German spies had reported to Hitler.

Stalin ordered thousands of freight trains to crisscross Russia. The trains stopped at every town and village. Men from sixteen to sixty jammed into freight cars. The trains brought them to the front, where they got a few days' training. Communist commissars injected them with a zeal to hurl back the invaders and save Mother Russia.

JULY 16: *With the German army near the town of Gomely, Russia*

M edical officer Heinrich Happe's Third Battalion had just swept through the insect-ridden Pripet Marshes. Happe and another German officer sipped captured Russian vodka in a tent and offered a toast. "Here's to the liberation of Russia from Godless communism and Christmas in the Kremlin."

"Why Christmas?" snapped the officer.
They could be there in weeks, he said. Moscow
sat only 300 miles away.

JULY 20: *A village near Smolensk, about 200 miles
from Moscow*

A Russian machine-gun nest sprayed advancing SS soldiers, halting their advance.
"These Russians are more stubborn fighters
than the French and British," a sergeant said
from behind a wall.

SS Major Rolf Scholtzberg sprawled behind
a wooden building. Another black-uniformed
SS officer crawled to Scholtzberg. "We've captured three commissars," he told Scholtzberg.

"Bring them here."

The three Communist Party leaders wore
beards. Their heads were shaven. They wore on
their sleeves the gold stars of commissars.

"You are people's commissars?" Scholtzberg asked in Russian.

The commissars looked surprised. "Yes.
Why?"

Scholtzberg motioned to an SS sergeant.
The sergeant drew a pistol, put the gleaming
barrel to the head of the first commissar, and
blew the unshaven head to bits. The sergeant
turned the gun to the heads of the other two
commissars. They were collapsing onto their
knees, shrieking, as he shot both.

Chapter Eight

AUG. 4: *German Group Center Headquarters, Russia*

General Halder told Hitler that the German army had destroyed 8,000 Russian tanks. But for every smashed tank, Halder said, the Russians sent two more.

Before the war, German officers estimated that the Russian army had four million soldiers. "Even after killing or capturing more than a million and half," Halder told Hitler ruefully, "we count almost six million—and more seem to be coming."

Hitler took a long, deep breath, then said, "Had I known they had as many tanks and men as that . . . I would never have taken the decision to attack."

AUG. 7: *Washington, the White House dining room*

The President guided his wheelchair toward the breakfast table. As he and his wife sipped coffee, the President said casually, "Well, I'm going to take some time off, Eleanor."

"Where are you going?"

"Oh, just a cruise off Cape Cod for some fishing."

AUGUST 8: *Cape Cod Canal*

Hundreds of people lined the banks to watch the President's yacht, the *Potomac*, cruise up the canal. They waved at the familiar figure of the President, wearing his blue Navy cape. As he waved, he held his cigarette holder at its usual rakish angle.

The crowds—and any German spies—waved at an actor. The real President Roosevelt had been carried off the *Potomac* during darkness. He now slept on the USS *Augusta* as the heavy cruiser whisked him to a meeting with a war leader he had never met.

AUGUST 9–12: *Placentia Bay, Newfoundland*

His Majesty's Ship *Prince of Wales* knifed through the flat waters of this Canadian bay. Standing on the battleship's bridge and wrapped in a sailor's blue pea coat, Winston Churchill could see the *Augusta* swing at anchor a mile off. As the *Prince of Wales* slid closer, the Prime Minister waved to the white-suited man he had crossed 3,000 miles of torpedo-infested Atlantic Ocean to meet for the first time.

An hour later, Churchill strode down the gangplank of the *Augusta*. He walked directly to the President and said, "At last we've gotten together."

Conferences began between their diplomats and military men. Churchill spoke openly about what he wanted most: the United States shooting at Hitler. He told Harry Hopkins: "I would rather have a declaration of war now and no supplies for six months than double the supplies you are sending us but no declaration of war."

Roosevelt frowned when he heard that. He told Hopkins that most Americans wanted England to win—but not at the cost of even one American soldier's life.

Churchill asked the President how he hoped to stop the Japanese drive into Southeast Asia. The pro-German Vichy-based French government had allowed Japan to march soldiers into Saigon, Hanoi, and Camranh Bay, bases in French Indochina. The Japanese now stood only a leapfrog jump from the British naval base at Singapore. If the Japanese took Singapore and the Philippines, Japan would own both the front door and the back door of Southeast Asia.

Roosevelt told Churchill that the Japanese got 80 percent of their fuel oil from the United States, and he had ordered that no more oil could be sent from the United States to Japan.

"Leave the Japanese to me, Winston," Roosevelt said. "I can baby them along for three months." After three months, the President said, the fuel tanks of Japan would stand empty. Their ships, tanks, and planes could not move anywhere.

Churchill and Roosevelt ended their shipboard conference with a statement broadcast to the world. The statement was called the Atlan-

tic Charter. It promised that "after the final destruction of the Nazi tyranny," a world orga-
nization—supported by the victors—would
stand as a policeman to keep peace.

AUGUST 23: *Wolf's Lair*
"Hitler is playing warlord again," Chief of
Staff Halder grumbled to General Hans
Guderian. The squat Guderian, with eyes like
bullet holes, had just landed after a hasty flight
from the Russian front. Guderian's tanks had
raced to within 200 miles of Moscow. But Hitler had decided to turn them away from Moscow and send them south instead. Guderian
hoped to change Hitler's mind.

"You are thinking, of course, of Moscow,"
Hitler said.

"Yes, my Führer. May I have permission to
give you my reasons?"

"By all means, Guderian."

Guderian told Hitler that Moscow was "the
head and heart of the Soviet Union . . . its political brain . . . the fall of Moscow will decide
the war." Capture Moscow, Guderian went on,
and Germans could winter in the warmth of
Moscow homes while the Russian army staggered backward to freeze in the arctic waste-
lands of Siberia.

"Let us march toward Moscow," Guderian
pleaded. "We shall take it."

"My generals," Hitler said with a knowing
smile, ". . . understand nothing of military ec-

onomics." To win a modern war, he said, an army needed to win oil and food while depriving the enemy of oil and food. Oil and grain in south Russia's Ukraine was feeding the Russian army. That oil and grain must be taken away from the Russians and fed to the German army.

A worried Guderian flew back to the front. A drive to the south would take weeks or months away from the capture of Moscow. He imagined his tanks caught in a bitter Russian winter only three months away—and he winced.

Chapter Nine

The German motorcycle troops roared through the town, rifles strapped across their backs. They were chasing Russians, whose trucks raised billows of dust as they sputtered up a road above the town.

Civilians watched the columns of German infantrymen streaming into the town. Men and women rushed out, throwing kisses, waving German flags. Like millions of other Russians, they welcomed the Germans as liberators who would lift from them Stalin's whip. None had read *Mein Kampf,* in which Hitler describes the Russians as a "mongrel race" suitable only for hard labor as slaves of the German "master race."

The blond, clean-cut Otto Ohlendorf, commanding officer of Special Action Group D, climbed out of his armored car. His helmeted troops leaped off trucks. Carrying light machine guns, they ran down streets, banging on doors of homes.

Three hours later, they had rounded up more than a hundred Jewish men, women, and children. Babies screamed in the arms of their mothers. Families were told to take from their houses only what they could carry.

"You will be resettled in another locality!" Ohlendorf shouted to the Jews. Eyes wide with fear, fathers, mothers, and children climbed into trucks. The Special Action troops packed the trucks tightly so the people stood shoulder to shoulder. The trucks roared out of the town.

Two miles away, the trucks stopped. The troops herded the Jews toward a deep ditch. Men, women, and children stood with their backs to the ditch, facing a row of heavy machine guns.

Screams ripped into the quiet, humid air. Ohlendorf dropped his hand. The blasts of the guns sent birds flapping upward from a nearby grove of trees. As though swiped backward by an invisible hand, the Jews toppled into the ditch. Minutes later, a truck shoveled dirt into the ditch to bury the dead and the moaning dying.

A German colonel asked Ohlendorf, "Why the children?"

"Our orders are that the Jewish population should be totally exterminated."

"Even the children?"

"Yes."

Special Action Group D was one of four extermination groups that trailed the army into Russia. So far, Special Action Group D had killed more than 40,000 commissars and Jews.

SEPTEMBER 4: *The Atlantic, near Iceland*

The USS *Greer* bobbed up and down in the steep waves. By Roosevelt's orders, U.S. warships trailed England-bound cargo ships almost halfway across the Atlantic. The destroyer's skipper, Lieutenant Commander Laurence Frost, watched as a British plane dropped depth bombs on a German U-boat whose periscope it had spotted.

The bombs rocked the U-boat. Its skipper saw the *Greer*, mistook it for English, and let loose a torpedo. Frost saw it coming and swerved, the torpedo missing. Then a second torpedo flashed by.

Frost decided to defend himself. "Drop depth charges!" shouted an officer. The depth bombs missed the sub, but the Americans had fired their first shot of World War II.

SEPTEMBER 9: *Washington, the Oval Office*

"We have sought no shooting war with Hitler," Roosevelt said in front of the microphones. He was giving a Fireside Chat by radio to Americans who had just read of the bombing of a German U-boat by the *Greer*. "We do not seek it now. But . . . when you see a rattlesnake poised to strike, you don't wait until he has struck before you crush him." From now on, he warned, any Axis warships that steamed within sight of patrolling American warships "do so at their own peril." Next day's newspapers called the Chat "Roosevelt's Shoot-on-Sight Speech."

SEPT. 10: *Aboard the battleship* Nagato, *off Japan*

Admiral Yamamoto knew why Rear Admiral Ryunosuke Kusaka, a trim naval aviation expert, had come on this visit. The navy's commander in chief, Admiral Nagano, still feared that Yamamoto's Pearl Harbor attack force would be detected and destroyed by the American navy.

Nagano had sent Kusaka to convince Yamamoto that his Pearl Harbor scheme was too risky.

Kusaka spoke bluntly. "You are an amateur naval strategist," he told Yamamoto. "Your ideas are not good for Japan. This operation is a gamble."

"I like games of chance," Yamamoto snapped. And, indeed, he loved to play poker by the hour.

He called staff officers to his cabin to prove that the plan was not as risky as Nagano and Kusaka believed. He and his officers pushed an argument that they believed tipped the scales toward a surprise attack. If the American Pacific Fleet were destroyed at Pearl Harbor, the United States would need years to build enough battleships and carriers to fight Japan. By then, Yamamoto told Kusaka, the Americans could not dislodge Japan from fortresses it would build in Southeast Asia.

"I will resign if Nagano turns down my plan," Yamamoto said.

SEPTEMBER 12: *Tokyo, headquarters of the naval commander in chief*

A dmiral Nagano listened as Kusaka told him of Yamamoto's threat to resign. Nagano knew that if Yamamoto resigned, admirals and generals would worry that Japan's rulers were taking the wrong course by going to war.

Nagano sighed. "If he has that much confidence," he said, "he must be allowed to carry on. We will attack Pearl Harbor!" He fixed a date: late November, but no later than early December.

SEPTEMBER 17: *Leningrad, northern Russia*

T wo German armies had cut off the city from the rest of Russia. Horse-drawn wagons clip-clopped across the ice of a nearby lake to bring in the only food for the city's three million people and its 200,000 defenders. Soldiers and civilians lived on a daily ration of a scrap of bread. Gaunt men, women, and children ate scraps of leather, carpenter's glue, even lipstick.

Yelena Skyrabina, a thirty-seven-year-old housewife, looked out a window and saw the stacks of emaciated corpses in the street. More than 11,000 had died in the last three weeks. Few people had the strength to bury their dead. Men, women, and children prowled the streets at night searching for food of any kind.

"It is so simple to die," Yelena wrote in her

diary. ". . . you lie on your bed and you never get up."

SEPTEMBER 28: *Berlin, Reich Chancellory*

"I told you so!" gloated Hitler. He waved reports from southern Russia in front of the nose of his commander in chief, General von Brauchitsch. Guderian's tanks had taken Kiev. That key city gave Hitler the oil and grain of the Ukraine. Two Russian armies had been wiped out and 600,000 prisoners rounded up.

The cowed von Brauchitsch nodded agreeably when Hitler called the victory "the greatest battle in the history of the world." Von Brauchitsch did not mention what the victory had cost: a month of warm weather while the army massed in front of Moscow waited for its spearhead, Guderian's tanks and armored divisions, to return.

Hitler knew that winter's icy blasts were only two months away. "Why hasn't Operation Typhoon started?" he shouted at von Brauchitsch. Typhoon was the code name for the attack on Moscow.

"It is impossible for Guderian and his Panzers to return so quickly," General Halder protested.

Hitler slammed a fist on the table. "Typhoon," he roared, "must begin no later than October second."

Chapter Ten

OCTOBER 2: *Moscow, the Kremlin*

Stalin studied a message from Richard Sorge, the German journalist in Tokyo who was a spy for Russia. "The Japanese," the message said, "are withdrawing the bulk of their troops from the Siberian-Manchurian border. They are assembling an army to invade to the south."

Stalin had posted more than a million winter-warfare troops, equipped with skis, along that border to fend off an attack by the Japanese. Stalin decided this time to believe Sorge. He ordered the winter-warfare troops rushed to Moscow.

OCTOBER 6: *Cologne, Germany*

SS soldiers used dog whips to drive the 6,000 Jewish families along the railroad tracks. Men, women, and children wore a large yellow Star of David sewn onto their clothing. Their faces were sunken and sallow. They had lived for most of the past year on half-rations in this Jewish ghetto. Now all ghettos in German cities were being emptied and the families "relocated." The German Ministry of Information in Berlin had announced the day before that there would be new "restrictive measures" against German Jews.

Holding babies and gripping children by the hand, bearded fathers and shawled mothers were crammed into hot, stinking freight cars. Soldiers slammed shut the doors as children begged on their knees for more light and air.

The freight trains jounced out of Cologne, headed for concentration camps in eastern Germany named Auschwitz and Bergen-Belsen.

A tall, professorial-looking lawyer, Adolf Eichmann, had been put in charge of Hitler's "Final Solution." One of Eichmann's aides watched the train leave. "The faster we get rid of them," he said to a soldier, "the better."

OCTOBER 10: *Orel, on the Smolensk-Moscow road*

Rain slashed across the face of General Guderian as he stood in the open hatch of the thirty-four-ton Mark IV tank. Guderian's tanks had come to within 150 miles of Moscow.

Guderian had just learned by radio that two German armies had encircled 660,000 Russians. Now only a few knots of Russian troops stood between Guderian and Moscow.

Guderian cursed the rain. A week of downpours had turned the road to mud. It sucked off of the calf-high boots of soldiers mushing through it. Black mud gripped the wheels of trucks so tightly that tanks had to pull them out. Guderian's tanks had charged eighty-five miles in one day before the rains struck. Now the mud's muck slowed him to six miles a day.

Each day, Guderian peered at a thermometer and saw a lower temperature. He had radioed Berlin, pleading for winter boots, socks, and overcoats.

His tank nosed out of Orel and turned east toward Moscow. The rain had stopped. It was beginning to snow.

OCTOBER 11: *The Bergen-Belsen concentration camp, Germany*

T he trains rolled into the camp from ghettos all across Germany. Freight cars were jammed with scarecrow bodies of Jewish men, women, and children who had survived days or weeks of near-suffocation locked inside.

Along routes to the camps, the freight cars were periodically opened so the Jews could throw out their dead. Some mothers hurled out live babies, hoping for the kindness of strangers.

Bergen-Belsen's SS guards, rifles slung on their shoulders, threw open the doors of the freight cars and flinched at the stench. They ordered the Jews to line up along the tracks. An orchestra of white-bloused schoolgirls came forward, playing polkas and waltzes on violins. Jews smiled hopefully. Maybe they really were being relocated to a place where they were welcome.

The soldiers escorted them to huge brick buildings that had no windows. Loudspeakers told the Jews to file inside and disrobe for showers and clean new clothes.

The Jews filed into large chambers. When a chamber was filled so that people stood shoulder to shoulder, the doors slammed shut behind them. Men, women, and crying children stared upward at a hissing sound coming from pipes in the ceiling. "Gas!" someone screamed, and then death came down, sucked into the lungs, leaving openmouthed corpses twisted and piled on one another.

Jewish prisoners dragged out the bodies. Under orders, they extracted gold teeth and cut off hair, which went to German factories to be converted into war materials.

OCTOBER 12: *Berlin, Ploetzensee Prison*

The Reverend Bernhard Lichtenberg, the graying dean of the Roman Catholic St. Hedwig's Church, had been brought here for questioning by the secret police. "Is it true, Father," a Gestapo man asked, "that you have publicly prayed for Jews?"

"I have."

Father Lichtenberg, the German Ministry of Information announced, would be sent to a concentration camp "for further interrogation."

OCTOBER 13: *Munich, Germany*

The latest issue of *Das Reich,* published by Josef Goebbel's Ministry of Propaganda, featured an article by the minister on why the new "restrictive measures" against Jews were being imposed.

"The fate of the Jews in Germany today," Goebbels wrote, "is indeed hard, but more than deserved. Recall the Führer's words of January 30, 1939, when he said, 'If world war comes, it will be the fault of the Jews and they will have to be exterminated.' "

Goebbels continued, "Jews are to be blamed for the war. Every Jew is our enemy, regardless of whether he is vegetating in a ghetto in Berlin or Hamburg or blaring the war trumpets in New York or Washington.

"If Jews ask you for help, show them immediately that you see through them and punish them by turning away and refusing even to speak to them. Jews have no right to passage among us as equals. When you see the Jewish Star of David, you see the man or woman marked as the people's enemy."

OCTOBER 23: *Tokyo, the Imperial Palace*

The fourteen delegates from the Imperial Conference sat on straight, hard chairs in two rows facing each other. Each delegate represented the army, navy, or the diplomatic service. Near the top of one line sat the mustached

General Hideki Tojo. The Emperor had just named Tojo to be the new prime minister.

With no more oil coming from America, Japan was reduced to a year's supply. Japan had only one other place to get that oil—Southeast Asia.

Tojo snuffed out a cigarette—one of fifty he chain-smoked daily—and rose to speak. He said he and the military had no desire to war against the might of America. "But we have to make a decision for war or peace," he said, "and we have to make that decision soon." The delegates nodded approvingly.

OCTOBER 24–26: *Moscow, Red Square*

S talin had ordered the lean-jawed, sarcastic General Georgi Zhukov to defend the city. Zhukov could muster only forty-five battalions. He needed 150. He told General Konstantin Rokossovsky, commanding the center of the Moscow line, "Stand to the death. Do not retreat a step."

Express trains raced into Moscow, whistles screeching. They carried more than a million troops from Siberia. Zhukov told their generals: "Stay on the far side of Moscow. I don't want the Germans to know you are here."

African-American soldiers gather at an Army base. Army units were all-black or all-white; there were no integrated units. These soldiers are wearing the peaked "Smokey the Bear" hats from World War I. These hats would soon vanish, replaced by caps with bills, or small cloth caps called "overseas hats." (*Washington, D.C., Public Library*)

OCTOBER 31: *Aboard the USS destroyer* Reuben James *between Iceland and Ireland*

Twenty-year-old sailor Leonidas Dickerson had just written to his aunt in Danville, Virginia, to tell her what life was like guarding convoys of cargo ships bound for Britain. By a secret order from the President, American warships now guarded convoys to Britain almost all the way across the Atlantic.

"We have gotten two subs, maybe more," Dickerson told his aunt.

Dickerson never saw the sub that sent a torpedo snaking through the ocean on this dark night. It blew up in the belly of the *Reuben James*. With red and yellow flames licking from its middle, the destroyer nosed downward to the ocean floor, carrying a hundred men and officers, Dickerson among them. The first American fighting men had died in World War II.

Chapter Eleven

Nov. 4: *Tokyo, Navy General Staff Headquarters*

The stocky, poker-faced General Tomoyuki Yamashita sat in the briefing room and wondered why the navy had called a dozen generals to this conference. General Yamashita commanded the 25th Japanese army. Sitting next to him was the sleepy-eyed General Masaharu Homma. If the Japanese invaded Southeast Asia, the navy would land Yamashita's army on beaches in British Malaya. Yamashita then had to fight through jungles to capture Singapore. The navy would land Homma in the Philippines.

The briefing began. Yamashita and Homma learned for the first time that while the navy ferried the armies southward the navy's airplanes would be bombing Pearl Harbor. Pearl Harbor! More than 3,000 miles from home! Even stony-faced Yamashita showed shock.

NOVEMBER 5: *Tokyo, the Imperial Palace*

After weeks of wrangling, the weary delegates to the Imperial Conference could not agree. Should they withdraw from Indochina in order to get oil from America? Or should they go to war and grab the oil in Southeast Asia? Tojo finally got the delegates to agree on a compromise: General Yamashita and General Homma would continue to prepare to conquer the Philippines and Malaya. Admiral Yamamoto would ready the task force to sail to Pearl Harbor. And a shrewd diplomat, Saburo Kurusu, would go to Washington to join Nomura and offer the Americans a package deal. The deal would trade oil from America for a promise from Japan to withdraw from Southeast Asia.

The generals and admirals howled objections. They couldn't get ready for war in a day if the Americans turned down the package deal. They needed a cutoff date when they had to be told if Japan was or was not going to war. Tojo set the date. Japan would decide on peace or war no later than November 30.

NOVEMBER 2: *Washington, Department of the Interior*

"There's been no real outrage among the American people about the torpedoing of the *Reuben James*," a friend said to Interior Secretary Harold Ickes.

"Because," growled Ickes, "Americans want war so little. We are in an age when we are more interested in movies and the radio and baseball and automobiles than in the fundamental truths of life."

NOVEMBER 13: *The Smolensk-Moscow road*

Guderian watched as one of his tanks, its metal treads screeching on rocks, yanked a truck out of a snowy ditch. The whipping wind and needling cold—the thermometer showed eight degrees below zero—pierced thin summer uniforms and turned arms blue. As many as 500 men in one regiment clumped through gales and snowdrifts with coal-black, frostbitten toes.

Moscow sat less than a hundred miles away from Guderian's tanks. But he saw growing panic among his troops as they plunged deeper into this winter-darkening, empty vastness. "Only those who saw the endless expanse of Russian snow . . . and felt the wind that blew across it, who drove for hour after hour through that no-man's-land only to find too-thin shelter with half-starved men," he would later write, could understand how this German army was weakening step by step on its way toward Moscow.

NOV. 17: *Aboard Vice Admiral Nagumo's flagship* Akagi, *at sea off Japan*

Its lights blacked out, the carrier plowed eastward. All task-force warships steered clear of shipping lanes, kept radio silence, and stayed tuned to Tokyo radio stations. The stations flashed weather reports to ships at sea, the reports laced with coded orders to Nagumo from

Admiral Yamamoto on his flagship anchored in Hiroshima Bay.

NOVEMBER 20: *The Smolensk-Moscow road*

Private soldier Benno Zieser's numbed hands gripped his Mauser rifle as he ran across the snowy field. He saw red flashes spurting from the woods a hundred yards away. Moments later, he heard the jackhammering roar of the Russian machine guns. He dived to the icy ground.

"Work your way forward!" Sergeant Vogt shouted.

Work your way forward! Like all infantrymen, Zieser dreaded that command. It meant crawling forward a few feet, then jumping up and running toward streams of bullets and hoping they would not tear apart a leg or an arm or half a torso.

"What a lot it needs to continually offer yourself as a target," Zieser later wrote in his diary. "Of your own free will, you give up your protective cover and trust to luck. Nobody wants to be the first to jump up . . . but nobody wants to lag behind as if he were milk livered. You just squeezed yourself into the ground, let off a couple of haphazard shots, and squinted at your neighbors to see how far ahead they are and if it's your turn next to get up and run forward."

Now it was his turn. He jumped up. He saw a man in front of him double up and seem to lay himself down—"forever," Zieser told himself. On all sides he heard the high-pitched cries of the wounded: "Stretcher bearer . . . For the name of God, over here . . . where's the stretcher bearer . . . here . . . over here!"

He flopped to the ground, thanking God nothing had hit him. Slugs ripped off tree branches above his head. He pressed his face into the earth, hoping his steel helmet covered all of his skull.

He heard the familiar *crump!* of an explosive, and this one shook the earth under him like a bowl of jelly.

"Mines! Mines!" The shouts came from all around him as others warned of land mines.

The explosions seemed to signal the Russian machine gunners to slip away into the forest. The machine guns stopped their infernal chattering. Zieser raised his head cautiously and heard someone screaming.

Zieser edged forward on his elbows, inch by inch. He scanned the ground for the telltale slivers of metal. He hated mines—they were almost impossible to see. Touch that sliver with your boot and one razor-sharp fragment could slice you straight up the backbone.

He saw that it was the giant Sergeant Vogt who was screaming. The mine had ripped off both his legs.

"Benno, my pistol, Benno . . ."

Zieser gingerly pulled the pistol from the sergeant's holster. Vogt's eyes begged Zieser to shoot him, but he suddenly flopped over on his side, stiffening in death. Breathing with relief, Zieser dropped the pistol to the ground.

Zieser noticed a motorcycle near the woods, smashed and turned upside down. He ran to the wreckage and saw a Russian woman soldier pinned under the motorcycle, a mass of dried blood where the socket of her right arm had been. Her eyes stared upward with a look of shock. Her motorcycle had run over one of her own mines.

NOVEMBER 20: *Washington, the State Department*

Ambassador Nomura led special ambassador Saburo Kurusu into the office of Cordell Hull.

Kurusu offered Hull the Imperial Council's deal. Japan would get all the oil it needed, most of it from the United States. In return, Japan would pull its troops out of southern Indochina. There would be no war.

NOVEMBER 21: *Washington, the War Department*

The Army's chief of staff, the jut-jawed, silver-haired General George Marshall, read a memo from Secretary Hull. The memo informed Marshall that Hull had made a generous counter-offer to keep the Japanese from going to war.

The U.S. would stop sending aid to China and would again ship aid to Japan. In return, the Japanese would not invade Southeast Asia.

Replying to Hull, Marshall wrote that the

Army and Navy were strongly for "the avoidance of war with Japan." America was not yet ready to fight both Japan and Germany, Marshall told Hull. Peace in the Pacific, he added, would help to ensure "the success of our war effort in Europe . . ."

NOVEMBER 25: *Washington, the Navy Department*

The Navy's Magic code breakers were reading every word coming from Tokyo to Nomura and Kurusu. The latest Magic intercept reported that Japan was doubling its number of troops in French Indochina. Knox phoned Hull and read the intercept to him.

The white-haired Hull exploded with a string of loud Tennessee-hillbilly expletives. "They're doubling their force—while those two Japs are telling me they'll pull out of Indochina if we give them oil and China."

The Japanese, Hull decided, really wanted war. He talked to President Roosevelt. Hull and Roosevelt drew up a new counterproposal to present to the Japanese. It said, in effect, we'll give you oil—but only if you get out of Southeast Asia.

Hull phoned Knox and said, "I have washed my hands of it," meaning his own deal to prevent war. "It is now in the hands of you and Stimson"—the Navy and the Army.

NOVEMBER 27: *Washington, the Navy Department*

Magic's crew had just decoded the latest message from Tokyo to Nomura and

Kurusu. The two envoys were told, "This time we mean it. The deadline [for the United States to accept a deal] absolutely cannot be changed." After that, "things are automatically going to happen." To American generals and admirals reading that message, Japan sounded like a nation readying for war.

General Marshall approved the sending of "war warning" messages to Admiral Kimmel and General Short in Hawaii.

NOVEMBER 27: *Washington, the Oval Office*

Ambassadors Nomura and Kurusu came smiling toward the President. But their smiles could not hide the shock they had felt minutes before when they read a note from Hull demanding that the Japanese get out of Southeast Asia—with no ifs, ands, buts, or deals. The ambassadors could not understand why Hull and Roosevelt had suddenly turned cold shoulders on any deal with Japan.

"You poured cold water on peace talks, Mr. President," Nomura said.

"I, too, am very disappointed," Roosevelt said. But, he went on, "cold water was poured on them [peace talks] when Japan occupied southern French Indochina. According to recent intelligences, there are fears [of] a second cold-water dousing . . ." The President stopped—he had come dangerously close to telling an enemy that he was reading its coded messages.

Chapter Twelve

DEC. 2: *Tokyo, Naval General Staff Headquarters*

The navy's commander in chief, Admiral Nagano, had just left Prime Minister Tojo, who told him, "The talks in Washington have ruptured—broken down." The November 30 deadline for military action had passed.

At 5:30 P.M. Tokyo time, a signal that used a special code was flashed to General Yamashita's headquarters ship, *Ryujo Muru,* one of hundreds of troopships streaming south toward the Philippines and Malaya. The same signal was beamed to Vice Admiral Nagumo's flagship, *Akagi,* as it pitched through waves a thousand miles from Pearl Harbor.

The signal was decoded and read: *Climb Mount Niitka.* Nagumo and Yamashita knew what the message really meant: *Let War Begin.*

DECEMBER 2: *Khimki, a suburb of Moscow*

The German scouts zoomed on their motorcycles down the icy, cobbled streets. They shot by rows of warehouses. Rifles suddenly blazed from the warehouse windows. The Germans wheeled their motorcycles to cover behind low walls. They pulled off the rifles strapped to their backs. Scurrying low to the ground, they ran to nearby houses and kicked in the doors. The houses were empty. The Germans poked their guns toward the snipers left by the retreating Russian rear guard. The snipers had faded away into the evening's dusk.

An officer told the soldiers to bed down here for the night. Tomorrow they would ride down the cobbled road straight into Moscow's Red Square. That evening, staring with binoculars from second-story windows, they could see the spires of the Kremlin eight miles away.

DECEMBER 3: *Wolf's Lair*

Hitler's hypnotic eyes glared at a wall map showing his three armies converging on Moscow, Guderian's Second Panzer Army clenched like a steel fist in the middle. Generals Halder and von Brauchitsch stood next to him. Hitler smiled. "One final heave," he said, "and we shall triumph."

Moscow would be the newest jewel captured by Hitler for his crown as the new emperor of Europe. His swastika would wave from the English Channel to Moscow. He could let England starve to death while he boasted that in only two and a half years he had won World War II.

DECEMBER 3: *Khimki, a suburb of Moscow*

Shortly after dawn, the German scouts saw waves of Russian men and women factory workers advancing up the cobbled streets. The workers gripped rifles and submachine guns. The scouts saw they were outnumbered, so they leaped on their motorcyles and raced back to join their battalion.

DECEMBER 4: *On the carrier* Akagi *in the Vacant Sea north of Hawaii*

Vice Admiral Nagumo stood on the bridge and stared back at his fan-shaped task force. Forty-foot waves thundered against prows and fifty-mile-an-hour winds whipped the sea. Nagumo now knew why few ships ventured through the Vacant Sea in December.

But he also felt the heavy burden lifting from his shoulders as his warships edged within a thousand miles of Pearl Harbor. No passing ships had seen them. Now he hoped no patrol planes would spot them.

DECEMBER 4: *Hickam Field, Oahu*

The PBY-4 Navy patrol plane taxied down the runway, turned, and sped off toward the southwest. Rear Admiral Patrick Bellinger watched the PBY become a speck in the sky.

Admiral Kimmel had ordered patrol planes to circle Oahu to spot Japanese submarines. If the Japanese declared war, the Navy feared that Japanese subs would lurk outside Pearl.

Bellinger had only a few patrol planes fit to fly. He told Kimmel that the planes patrolled to the south and west, the two most likely approaches from Japan. No one thought that the enemy would come from the wild sea to the north.

DECEMBER 4: *A briefing room aboard the* Akagi

Two of Admiral Yamamoto's chief officers in planning the Pearl Harbor attack had been the sharp-featured, tiny (five-foot-three) Minoru Genda and the trim, natty Mitsuo Fuchida. Commander Genda had flown dive-bombers in China. Commander Mitsuo Fuchida flew Zeros, becoming Japan's leading ace.

For the past three months, Genda and Fuchida had trained the pilots who would fly the task force's 355 dive-bombers, high-level bombers, and fighters for the attack on Pearl Harbor. This would be the final briefing.

"We will launch the first attack about two hundred and thirty miles north of Oahu," Fuchida told the pilots. The planes would attack in two waves.

Genda explained that Fuchida would lead the first wave. If he saw that the Americans were caught by surprise, he would shoot a flare from his cockpit. That would signal the dive-bombers that they could come in low without fear of ack-ack fire.

Fuchida would then break radio silence, calling out, *"Tora! Tora! Tora!"* ("Tiger! Tiger! Tiger!"). That would signal the second wave that the fleet sat defenseless, sitting ducks for Japanese bombs and torpedos.

DECEMBER 6: *Honolulu, Japanese Consulate*

The Japanese spy, Takeo Yoshikawa, had just returned from a final taxi ride to check the Pacific Fleet from his favorite perch overlooking the naval base. Late at night, he sent a coded cable to Tokyo.

Most of the fleet's ships, he reported, sat in their berths, as Admiral Yamamoto had hoped. Only the carriers *Enterprise* and *Lexington* and two battleships were at sea. Yoshikawa said he had observed nine battleships, eight light cruisers, and seventeen destroyers.

DECEMBER 6: *Aboard the* Akagi *within 400 miles of Oahu*

Radio Tokyo broadcast hourly weather reports to Japanese ships at sea. Admiral Yamamoto ordered Radio Tokyo to add a brief item to each weather broadcast. Hidden in those items were coded messages to the task force, which still kept its radio transmitters silent. One radioed word would tip off their location to American eavesdroppers.

Commander Fuchida scanned the latest coded message. It told him what the spy Yoshikawa had observed, that most of the Pacific Fleet had not left Pearl Harbor.

DECEMBER 6: *Washington, the Navy Department*

On this cold, dank Saturday morning, Magic's code breakers frowned as they bent at their desks to scan messages sent from Tokyo to its army and navy. For a week the messages had told them that a huge Japanese naval armada with troop transports was sailing southward, destination unknown. The Navy guessed that this was the start of the long-expected Japanese invasion of Southeast Asia, the British base at Singapore in Malaya being the prime target.

That information told Magic's men and women the location of half the Japanese navy. Where was the other half? No messages had been sent to or from ships like the *Akagi* for weeks. Where were they?

DECEMBER 6, 6 P.M.: *Washington, Japanese Embassy*

The teletype machine clattered, its typewriter printing a message coming in from Tokyo. The message, in code, was a fourteen-part reply to Hull's demand that Japan get out of Southeast Asia. The message began with instructions to Nomura and Kurusu: Deliver this to Cordell Hull at 1 P.M. tomorrow afternoon, December 7. That would be 8 A.M. in the morning, Pearl Harbor time. Clerks began to decode and translate the first thirteen parts of the reply. The fourteenth part had not yet come in.

DECEMBER 6, 7 P.M.: *Washington, the Navy Department*

Magic operators busily decoded the first thirteen parts of the message from Tokyo. A Navy officer raced by car to the White House with a copy.

DECEMBER 6, 8 P.M.: *A White House study*

The President was poring over his stamp collection, which he had put together since boyhood. His closest aide, Harry Hopkins, slouched on a couch in the corner. Roosevelt read the thirteen parts of the Japanese message to Hull, which told the United States to mind its own business. Japan would do what it wanted in Southeast Asia. And it said it was ending all talks between its ambassadors and the U.S. State Department.

Roosevelt tossed the sheafs of paper toward Hopkins and said, "This means war."

"Too bad we can't strike the first blow," said Hopkins.

"No, we can't," the President said. "We are a democratic and a peaceful people."

DECEMBER 6: *Klin, ten miles from Moscow*

Lieutenant Rostilav Gorbunov dashed inside the shattered schoolhouse. His company of infantry—150 riflemen and machine gunners, scurried after him, their helmeted heads down. The pursuing German tanks were firing shells that hit the snowy ground of the schoolhouse lawn, throwing up clods of dirt that clattered down on the Russian helmets.

"Battalion's orders are no retreat from here," Gorbunov told the men inside a schoolroom. He decided not to tell about the rocket. After all, having been chased for months from town to town, what Soviet soldier would believe that he might soon chase instead of being chased?

The machine gunners set up their weapons on the second floor of the schoolhouse. The riflemen hunched behind windows on the first floor. Snow whirled heavily outside, whipping through gaping holes in the walls.

The men talked loudly of that afternoon's house-to-house street battles. "I said, 'Surrender, you,' " one soldier was saying.

"Did you let him have it?"

"He was so scared his gun was fluttering like a fan."

"Did you let him have it?" the other soldier asked impatiently.

"Well," said the first soldier hesitantly, "if he doesn't surrender, you got to—"

"You said it," broke in Ivan Kochesov, a burly bus driver from southern Russia. "That's what I do—I let them have it!"

Gorbunov moved from room to room, peering from behind the men's shoulders to check their zones of fire. A soldier hissed and pointed to a line of dark figures sliding down into the gully.

"Open fire!"

More than a hundred gun muzzles blasted at once, their reverberations shaking pictures off the walls of the schoolrooms.

"Our ammunition is running low, Lieutenant," a machine gunner shouted above the din.

A roar suddenly filled Gorbunov's head as he skidded across the floor.

"Direct hit in the back of the building with a mortar shell!" he heard someone say. Staggering to his feet, he saw blood stream down the floor from the rooms in the rear. Screams pierced the blasting sounds of the guns.

Germans swarmed down the slope. Gorbunov grabbed a dead man's tommy gun and waved it like a garden hose as he fired into the advancing Germans. Bodies leaped, twisted, whirled, and vanished.

A sergeant pounded Gorbunov's shoulder. Gobunov realized that the tommy gun had run out of bullets. He reached down and grabbed another ammo disc when the red flame caught his eye.

A red rocket was flaring in the southwest sky, blossoming out like a crimson flower.

The counterattack! The battalion colonel had told Gorbunov and his other officers that morning: If you see that red rocket in the southwest, counterattack!

Gorbunov ran down the stairs, gripping the tommy gun. Only about half the riflemen were still firing; the others were dead or dying.

"Follow me!" he yelled. He ran out the door, not looking back, the tommy gun jumping in his hands as he fired from his hip.

Loud popping sounds made him whirl. Two Germans writhed screaming on the ground behind him. One of his riflemen had cut them down with a burst. His platoon surged behind him through the thickening snow. They charged up the slope, hurling grenades.

DECEMBER 6: *Moscow Defense Headquarters*

"Are the red rockets rising by now all along the two hundred miles of Moscow front?" General Zhukov asked. Yes sir, an aide told the pale Zhukov, who had not slept in three nights.

The signal was supposed to unleash a counterattack by two million troops, more than a million the winter-warfare fighters from Siberia whom Zhukov had kept in reserve, hidden and rested.

DECEMBER 6: *A village twenty miles from Moscow*

General Guderian stood high on his command tank. He watched the line of Russian T-34 tanks, as tall as two-story buildings, crush German troops in their holes. Artillery officers shouted at crews to fire antitank guns—but the guns sat silent. The twenty-below-zero cold had frozen firing mechanisms.

"Panic," he told an aide, "has reached a hundred miles to the rear." That night, he telegraphed General Halder: "What happened today is a warning that the combat ability of our infantry is at an end."

DECEMBER 7: *The Moscow-Smolensk road*

Guderian issued the order for his army to retreat—the first order to retreat ever heard by an army of Hitler.

DECEMBER 7: *The Moscow-Smolensk road*

Private soldier Zieser saw one wave of the Siberian winter troops zoom on skis down the slope. They wore white hooded parkas and poured streams of armor-piercing bullets from submachine guns.

Shells pounded all around Zieser and his company. "Siberians . . . they're encircling us from the rear . . . ," an officer shouted.

Zieser turned and ran, ignoring the pain in his frostbitten feet. Men crumpled and dropped in front of him. His company was no longer in retreat, Zieser told himself. This was a panicky rout.

DECEMBER 7: *Wolf's Lair*

Hitler raged. Only a week ago, his armies had grasped Moscow by the throat. Now Hadler was telling him that Guderian, Beck, and Kluge were retreating, even fleeing, from Zhukov's counterattack. That sudden charge of a million fresh troops had shocked Hitler's generals, who thought they had drained the Russian bear of all its blood.

"Remain where you are and retreat no farther!" Hitler stormed. "It is better to fight and die than to retreat and die!"

But his once-all-conquering soldiers stum-

bled through waist-high snow and freezing
winds pursued by the Russian army.

DEC. 7, 3 A.M.: *Aboard the aircraft carrier* Kaga

Seaman Iki Kuramoto sat in his hammock in
the cramped quarters below deck. A pilot
had just told him that the task force had come
to bomb Hawaii. "A dream come true," he
wrote to his mother. "what will the people at
home think when they hear the news!" And
then he summed up a century of hatred toward
the Europeans who had invaded the Orient:
"We will teach the arrogant Anglo-Saxon
scoundrels a lesson!" he wrote.

DECEMBER 7, 8:40 A.M.: *Washington, the Japanese
Embassy (3:40 A.M. Pearl Harbor time)*

The clerks had finished decoding and trans-
lating the fourteenth section of the reply to
Hull. A typist hastily began to retype the entire
message. Nomura and Kurusu phoned Hull
and asked to meet him at the State Department
at 1 P.M. Neither knew why the meeting had to
be—as Tokyo directed—at 1 P.M. (8 A.M. Pearl
Harbor time) on a Sunday afternoon. Tokyo
had not told their two envoys about the Pearl
Harbor attack.

DECEMBER 7, 9 A.M.: *Washington, the Navy
Department (4 A.M. Pearl Harbor time)*

The fourteenth section had just been decoded by Magic. The Navy's intelligence

officers discussed why the message had to be delivered to Hull at 1 P.M. on a Sunday. The officers concluded, as one said, "that the Japanese were going to attack some American installation in the Pacific area." But which one? Certainly not Pearl Harbor. The Navy believed—wrongly—that after receiving General Marshall's war warning, Admiral Kimmel had ordered the Pacific Fleet to sea.

A Magic officer phoned admirals and generals to alert them to Magic's suspicions. He talked to General Marshall, who had been horseback riding. Marshall said he would read the message later in the morning.

DECEMBER 7, 4:30 A.M.: *Aboard the* Akagi, *220 miles north of Pearl Harbor*

Vice Admiral Nagumo asked Commander Genda to come to the bridge. "I have brought the task force successfully to the point of attack," a relieved Nagumo told Genda. "From now on, the burden is on your shoulders and the rest of the flying group."

"Admiral," Genda said, "I am sure that the airmen will succeed."

Genda went below and met Fuchida, who was buckling on his airman's uniform over long red underwear. "Hawaii still sleeps," Fuchida said.

"How do you know?"

"The Honolulu radio station still plays soft music."

DECEMBER 7, 6 A.M.: *Aboard the* Akagi

Commander Fuchida walked toward his three-man bomber, the first that would take off. A crewman handed him a white scarf marked *"Hissho"* ("Certain Victory"). "This is from *Akagi's* crew," the sailor said. "We would like you to carry this to Pearl Harbor on our behalf."

Fuchida bound the scarf around his helmet.

DECEMBER 7, 11:30 A.M.: *Washington, the Japanese Embassy (6:30 A.M. Pearl Harbor time)*

A new typist had made so many mistakes that the entire Tokyo message had to be retyped. An embarrassed Nomura phoned Hull and asked that their meeting be postponed until 2 P.M.

DECEMBER 7, 7 A.M.: *11,000 feet over the Pacific, 150 miles from Pearl Harbor*

Strapped in the observer's seat of the Katy bomber, Fuchida looked back at the V-shaped formations of some 180 bombers as they snarled southward. The second wave, another 175 bombers and fighters, was slowly rising from the six aircraft carriers. The rising sun broke between clouds, flashing streams of gold light across the blue Pacific. "What a glorious dawn for Japan!" Fuchida said to himself.

DECEMBER 7, 7:15 A.M.: *U.S. Army radar station, north Oahu*

Privates Joseph Lockard and George Elliott watched bleeps become larger on the radar screen. "There must be fifty planes coming in," Elliott said.

He marked the planes at 132 miles from Oahu. Lockard phoned an officer, telling him: "They are the biggest sighting I've ever seen on radar."

"That's a group of B-17s flying in from California," the officer said. "Don't worry about it."

Lockard hung up. He had not told the officer that at least fifty planes showed on the screen. If he had, an air-raid alert might have rung. The entire Army Air Corps did not have many more than fifty B-17s.

DECEMBER 7, 7:40 A.M.: *10,000 feet over Oahu*

Fuchida blinked at the sight that glittered in the morning sun. He saw the eight battleships lined up in a row, shining like long pieces of silver.

And their decks were empty, their guns unmanned. Fuchida fired a pistol rocket, its flare telling the dive-bombers behind him that they could swoop low to unleash their torpedoes. No one had seen them coming.

DECEMBER 7, 7:53 A.M.: *5,000 feet over Oahu*

Fuchida broke the task force's radio silence to tell the second wave, as well as the nervous crews aboard ships, that a daring scheme had caught the Americans literally asleep. He radioed the triumphant code words: *"Tora! Tora! Tora!"*

DECEMBER 7, 8 A.M.: *On the decks of the Japanese task force:*

Sailors wept. Officers and crewmen reached out to clasp hands. And their shouts resounded over the Pacific swells: *"Tora! Tora! Tora!"*

DECEMBER 7, 8:05 A.M. TO 10:20 A.M.

DECEMBER 7, *An Oahu golf course*

Two admirals saw the red ball on the fuselage of the low-flying dive bomber and mistook it for the red star on Russian planes. Standing at a tee, one admiral looked up and said, "Why doesn't anyone tell me anything around here? I didn't know we'd invited the Russians for fleet maneuvers."

DECEMBER 7: *Aboard the battleship* California

Lieutenant Commander M. N. Little saw a plane peel off from formation and turn toward him. He watched the foam-white track of a torpedo weave toward the battleship. It shot by the *California*'s prow and exploded a hundred yards away, throwing up an avalanche of water onto the *California*'s decks.

DECEMBER 7: *Aboard the battleship* Arizona

A sailor, W. W. Parker, sat watch on the top deck. He stared, eyes wide with admiration, at what he thought were American planes practicing dive-bomb runs. He watched one plane race toward him, so far below him that its

This picture of Pearl Harbor was taken by a Japanese plane as it came in to drop its bombs on the morning of December 7. Water shoots skyward near Battleship Row as the Japanese plane that dropped the bomb circles away. *(National Archives)*

propeller seemed to touch the water.

When the torpedo hit, the giant ship rolled heavily to one side. The torpedo slanted downward, exploding between the ship's boiler rooms and the ammunition holds.

DECEMBER 7: *2,000 feet above Pearl Harbor*

Commander Fuchida saw the bolt of white light flash upward from the *Arizona*. Next came an eruption of smoke—black and blood red. The shock waves shook his bomber. He saw hundreds of oil-black heads bobbing in the waters all around the ship.

DECEMBER 7: *Pearl Harbor Naval Yard*

The voice of Air Operations Commander Logan Ramsey boomed out over dockside loudspeakers: "Air raid, Pearl Harbor! This is no drill! This is no drill! Repeat! This is . . ."

DECEMBER 7: *At the* Arizona*'s berth*

Tongues of fire leaped out from below the decks, setting aflame the oily water. The licking red flames burned men hurled from their bunks, some alive and thrashing in the water, others dying with torn bodies, others staring face upward.

The *Arizona* began to sink slowly into the harbor's mud.

DECEMBER 7: *Aboard the* Arizona

Seaman S. F. Bowen ran across the flaming deck, its steel plates so hot his shoelaces began to burn. He looked up to see a hunk of white-hot metal, as big as a basketball, plunge from a mast and crash through the deck. Moments later, the deck reached water level. The seawater swept over sizzling steel. Clouds of blinding steam billowed upward and then the first deck went under water. The *Arizona* slipped downward until only its masts showed. Below its decks, more than a thousand dead men were forever entombed.

DECEMBER 7: *Ford Island, Pearl Harbor*

Hundreds of burned and bleeding men swam or drifted onto the beach. Navy medics were pulling up in their cars. They injected morphine to dull the pain of sailors screaming with blistered, torn flesh. Mary Ann Ramsey, a sixteen-year-old officer's daughter, cradled in her arms sailors crying for their mothers. She murmured softly to them until they died. She covered each dead man and moved on to the next one.

DECEMBER 7: *On a torpedo bomber streaking toward the battleship* Oklahoma

Lieutenant Jinichi Goto aimed the Katy straight at the *Oklahoma*'s hull, skimming forty feet above the water. The *Oklahoma*'s hull grew larger and larger in front of Goto, an expanding gray wall. He pressed the yellow button to release the torpedo. He pulled up, the plane zooming below the ship's crow's nest.

DECEMBER 7: *Aboard the battleship* Oklahoma

Goto's torpedo and five others rammed into the ship's hull within five minutes. The 30,000 tons of steel flopped onto its port side, water rushing across its lower decks. Commander Jesse Kenworthy's command crackled over loudspeakers: "Abandon ship!"

Lurching toward a ladder below decks, seaman George Murphy wondered why the ceiling was white-tiled. Moments later, he realized he was looking up at the operating-room floor.

Water poured through truck-size rips in the hull. *Oklahoma* turned bottom up, her steel masts long poles stuck into the harbor's mud. Hundreds of sailors and officers slithered down her slippery-sided hull.

Inside the upside-down hull, 125 men grappled in shoulder-deep water, trapped in a sealed chamber. They sucked at corners to breathe pockets of air. Only thirty-two would find enough air to be brought out alive a day and a half later.

DECEMBER 7: *On a dive-bomber 500 feet above Battleship Row*

Lieutenant Seizo Ofuchi began his dive at the battleship *West Virginia*. His nerves, he realized, "were numbed and . . . I just gave myself over to fate." He dropped the bomb, turned the plane, and saw antiaircraft shells burst around him in big black puffs. As he leveled off the plane, he said later, "I really got scared."

DECEMBER 7: *2,000 feet above Pearl Harbor*

Commander Fuchida's bomber zoomed over Battleship Row. Orange flame licked upward and black smoke billowed from one end of the row to the other. The *Arizona* had sunk to her superstructure. The *Oklahoma* had turned over. Flames roared through the *West Virginia* and the *Tennessee*. The *California* was listing sharply, fires a hundred feet high blazing from bow to stern.

DECEMBER 7: *A gun turret on the cruiser* New Orleans

Explosions blew out lights and the electrical system for loading shells into ack-ack guns. Groping in the steamy darkness, sailors and officers formed human chains to pass shells to the gunners' mates. Among the bare-chested, grimy men stood Chaplain Howell Forgy, who prayed for dead, dying, and fighting Americans while he grabbed shells and chanted, "Praise the Lord and pass the ammunition!"

DECEMBER 7: *Below decks of the* California

Water flooded into the hold where machinist's mate Robert Scott hand-pumped a compressor to feed air to the ship's big guns. "Get out!" a sailor told Scott. "Water is pouring in!"

"I'll stay here and give them air as long as the guns are going," Scott said. A sudden wave of water panicked a sailor. He slammed shut a watertight door. The trapped Scott kept pumping the compressor until he drowned.

DECEMBER 7: *Pacific Fleet Headquarters*

Admiral Kimmel arrived. Intelligence officers told him they were guessing that the planes came from one or two aircraft carriers that had probably approached from the west.

As Kimmel studied a chart, a Zero fighter dived at the building. A machine-gun bullet skipped over the ground, pinged through a window, and then, spent, hit Kimmel harmlessly in the chest. The slug dropped to the floor. Kimmel stared at it and muttered, "Too bad it didn't kill me."

DECEMBER 7: *300 feet above Bellows Air Base*

Lieutenant Fuista Iida looked down from the cockpit of his Zero and saw rows of American bombers and fighters parked wing tip to wing tip. He skimmed over the runway, spraying bullets. P-40 fighters and B-17 Flying Fortresses burst into flame.

Iida saw a sailor standing in front of a building, gripping a rifle and pumping single shots at his Zero from no more than 300 feet away. Iida veered the roaring 300-mile-an-hour fighter straight at the rifleman, six machine guns blazing slugs heavy enough to blow holes in bombers.

The Zero's slugs pockmarked a wall behind aviation ordnance man Tom Sands. He did not move, snapping off bullets. As the Zero zoomed ten feet over his head, its guns suddenly stopped firing. The Zero wobbled out of control, smashed into a road, skidded, and tore apart its fuselage and the body of its dead pilot.

DECEMBER 7: *Wheeler Air Base*

Air Corps lieutenants Kenneth Taylor and George Welch had leaped into their P-40s soon after the air raid began. They flew north, saw no Japanese planes, then landed at Wheeler to refuel. A dozen Zeros flashed out of the morning sun and swept over the field, their guns tattooing parked planes.

Taylor, Welch, and a half-dozen other pilots rammed their fighters upward. Welch saw a

Zero hanging on Taylor's rear. He put the Zero in his sights and traced a row of holes across its fuselage. The Zero coughed flame and smoke and spiraled downward into the sea. It was the first of seven Zeros that Taylor and Welch would blow out of the sky in the next sixty minutes.

DECEMBER 7: *5,000 feet over Pearl Harbor*

Commander Fuchida could no longer see Battleship Row, black smoke clouding his view. But he could see ack-ack bursts throwing ink-black clouds all around the second wave of attacking planes. Fighters and ack-ack, he knew, had downed at least a dozen of his planes. Now, almost exactly two hours after he had arrived over Pearl, he rocked his wings, the signal for all planes to return to their carriers. When he saw the last plane a pinpoint to the north, he ordered his pilot to speed back to the *Akagi*.

He left behind "success beyond our wildest dreams." His planes had sunk, capsized, or damaged eighteen ships of the Pacific Fleet. Thirty-four Navy bombers and fighters had been destroyed. The U.S. Air Corps had lost four of its scarce Flying Fortresses, the world's heaviest bomber, plus twelve other bombers and fifty-nine of its best fighters. Oahu's five air bases sat riddled, smoking, and burying their dead.

Smoke billows from the battleships that were hit by Japanese bombs as they were anchored in Pearl Harbor. Some of Japan's leaders, like Prime Minister Tojo, thought that Americans would be so stunned by the attack that they would lack the will to fight. They did not understand that such a sneak attack would make most Americans fighting mad. *(National Archives)*

Within two hours, 2,403 Americans had died, and another 1,178 were wounded. Japan lost twenty-nine planes, and fifty men were dead or wounded.

DECEMBER 7, 10:20 A.M.: *Aboard the* Akagi

Commander Fuchida leaped out of his bomber and snapped orders to refuel all planes. He told pilots to prepare for a third attack.

Commander Genda said no. Surprise had gone, Genda told Fuchida. A third wave would be blasted out of the sky.

Fuchida implored Genda. One more strike would break the back of the Pacific Fleet. Japan would win the war on its first day with one last blow.

Genda still said no. Fuchida ran to the bridge and pleaded with Admiral Nagumo for one final assault.

Nagumo had nervously scanned the skies all during these two hours. He feared seeing the prows of the carriers *Enterprise* and *Lexington* poke over the horizon. A mass attack by hundreds of planes from the two carriers and the B-17s on Oahu would overwhelm his fighters and cripple the ships that were not destroyed.

Nagumo had taken a gigantic gamble by steaming half the Imperial Navy into the teeth of the American Navy. He had won, his losses far cheaper than he had expected. But he did not care to gamble a second time. There would be no third wave. The task force turned west to Japan.

DECEMBER 7, 1:47 P.M.: *Washington, the Oval Office (8:47 A.M., Pearl Harbor time)*

The President had just finished lunch at his desk. He was feeding scraps to his little black dog, Fala, when the phone rang. The caller was Navy Secretary Frank Knox, who said in his spluttering way, "Mr. President, it looks like the Japanese have attacked Pearl Harbor."

"NO!" The President's shocked voice was so loud that Harry Hopkins, lounging on a sofa, came to his feet.

Roosevelt dialed Cordell Hull, knowing the secretary of state was meeting the Japanese at 2 P.M. He told Hull what Knox had told him.

DECEMBER 7, 2:05 P.M.: *Washington, the State Department*

Nomura and Kurusu entered Hull's office. He did not offer them chairs. He asked why Tokyo had wanted them to meet at 1 P.M. "I do not know," Nomura said. Hull read the message from Tokyo. He knew the words were now meaningless. Without declaring war, Japan had attacked America. World War II had now spread around the globe.

Hull dismissed the ambassadors, who walked hangdog out of the office. When the door shut, the country-boy anger shot out of the mouth of the silver-haired Tennessean: "Scoundrels."

DECEMBER 7: *New York City, the Polo Grounds*

The Brooklyn Dodgers led the New York Giants, 14–7, in the second quarter of a National Football League pro game. In the press box, a reporter stared at a stuttering teletype machine and said, "How do you like this upset—the Cards are beating the Bears by one touchdown."

Minutes later, someone else looked at the machine and shouted, "Oh, my God!"

"The Cards score again?" someone asked.

"No. The Japs have attacked Pearl Harbor."

DECEMBER 7: *Washington, the Senate*

The gray-haired Michigan senator Arthur Vandenberg had led isolationists in battling to keep America out of war. After hearing of the attack, he wrote in his diary that December 7, 1941, had "ended isolationism for any realist."

DECEMBER 7: *Washington, the Oval Office*

Roosevelt told the assembled leaders of Congress that he would address a joint session of Congress the next day and ask for a declaration of war against Japan. When they left, he called in Grace Tully.

He began to dictate to her the speech to Congress. He spoke as calmly, Grace thought, as if dictating any ordinary letter:

"Yesterday comma December 7 comma 1941 dash a date which will live in infamy dash . . ."

DECEMBER 7: *Santa Cruz, California*

Coast Guard men, carrying rifles and pistols, knocked on beach-house doors and ordered more than a thousand people to evacuate their homes. "The Japs might hit the beaches at any time," the Coast Guard men said.

DECEMBER 7: *Twenty-five miles off San Diego*

The skipper of Japanese submarine *I-10* could see the city's glow on the eastern horizon. His orders were to await orders before sinking merchant vessels. *I-10* was one of nine Japanese submarines hanging under water between Seattle and San Diego. They hoped to strike at U.S. warships that might rush to the Pacific Fleet at Pearl Harbor.

DECEMBER 7: *Beverly Hills, California*

Hundreds of Japanese families worked for movie people as maids, cooks, and gardeners. As night fell, the Japanese chattered among themselves. All day long, their bosses had thrown hard, even angry glances at them. Radio broadcasts warned Americans to be alert for spying and sabotage by Japanese aliens.

The attack on Pearl Harbor changed the minds of Americans who did not want the country fighting in its second world war in twenty-three years. This poster, a carryover from the First World War, brought hundreds of men to recruiting stations on Monday, December 8. *(Library of Congress)*

DECEMBER 8: *Chicago, State Street*

Men lined up before dawn to enlist in the Army and Navy. Many talked about where they had been the day before when they heard of the attack. Few of their generation would ever forget where they were that day and what they were doing.

Other Americans had begun to hum the first lines of a song that would soon be on the Hit Parade:

> *Let's remember Pearl Harbor*
> *As we go to meet the foe . . .*

DEC. 8: *Manila, the home of General Douglas MacArthur*

The phone rang in the bedroom. General Douglas MacArthur reached groggily over his sleeping wife to grab the phone. The time was about four in the morning Manila time, early afternoon of December 7 in Washington.

Four months earlier, President Roosevelt had appointed Lieutenant General Douglas MacArthur as the commander of the Filipino and American troops guarding the Philippines.

Calling on the phone was MacArthur's chief of staff, General Dick Sutherland. "The Japs are attacking Pearl Harbor," he told MacArthur.

MacArthur had expected an attack on the Philippines. But he had not expected an attack on America's fortress in the Pacific. "Pearl Harbor!" he exclaimed, amazement in his voice. "That should be our strong point."

He dressed quickly, summoned his chauffeur, and drove in his dusty Packard to his headquarters.

DECEMBER 8: *Manila, MacArthur's headquarters*

Four hours had now gone by since the attack on Pearl Harbor. Dozens of colonels and generals milled around outside MacArthur's office, waiting to see the general and wondering what to do next.

Among the officers was the chunky Brigadier General Lewis Brereton, commander of MacArthur's air force. He told the chief of staff, Dick Sutherland, that he had to see the general. Sutherland told him that lots of people wanted to see the general. He would just have to wait his turn.

Brereton paced the floor nervously. The entire U.S. Army Air Corps had fewer than 100 B-17 Flying Fortresses, the world's biggest bomber. Thirty-five had been sent to Clark Field here on the island of Luzon in the Philippines. The B-17s could bomb Japanese troopships striking at the Philippines.

Earlier this month, after getting the war warning from Washington, MacArthur told the B-17 pilots to fly the bombers from Luzon to another island in the Philippines. Luzon sat too close to the Japanese fighter bases on the island of Formosa. MacArthur wanted the B-17s moved out of fighter range.

But, unknown to MacArthur, eighteen of the Flying Fortresses were parked on Luzon's Clark Field, lined up wing to wing. Brereton wanted to warn MacArthur that half of his air force still sat under the shadow of Japanese bombs.

General Brereton again pleaded to see MacArthur. The bossy Sutherland said no, he would have to wait his turn. Hours ticked by. Finally, Brereton decided that he would order the B-17 pilots to take off for a safe island.

DECEMBER 8: *Luzon, Clark Field*

As General Brereton arrived to order the B-17s to leave, radar showed a wave of Japanese planes approaching. Brereton ordered the unarmed bombers to take off and circle out of range of the Japanese fighters.

The Japanese Zeros swooped, strafed Clark, then soared away. Brereton ordered the B-17s down.

As the bombers lumbered down the runway, a second wave of Zeros swept over Clark. They poured shells into the defenseless B-17s. And they riddled fighters that tried to lift off to protect the bombers. B-17s blew up, orange and black balls of smoke and flame littering the runway. In just a few minutes, half of America's Far East bomber fleet was wiped out. Japanese troopships could sail toward Manila and the Philippines with much less fear that American bombers would blow them to bits.

DECEMBER 10, *Tobruk, North Africa*

Field Marshal Rommel looked back at the rapidly receding buildings of Tobruk, his tank grinding through the desert sand toward Libya. A series of bloody tank battles against the newly organized British Eighth Army (successors to the Army of the Nile) had cost Rommel 33,000 killed, wounded, or captured Afrika Korps soldiers and almost half his 600 tanks.

Rommel had decided to retreat and refit his battered troops in Tripoli.

As Rommel rode away, the Rats of Tobruk streamed out into the desert. For almost a year they had kept Rommel away from the water he needed to conquer Egypt. One Tobruk commander sent a message to Cairo: "Tobruk is relieved, but not as relieved as I am."

DECEMBER 11: *The Jitra Line, Malaya*

General Yamashita stood in the rain, his boots sinking almost to his knees in jungle mud. He studied a map that showed the forts of the Jitra Line. The British had built the Jitra Line to protect its island naval base at Singapore some one hundred miles to the south. British generals had bragged that the Jitra Line would hold back invaders for three months.

An officer ran up and saluted Yamashita. The Jitra Line, the officer said, had been smashed.

"So soon?" asked an amazed Yamashita.

"In fifteen hours," the officer said.

Yamashita had used only 500 of his 10,000-man invasion force to roll over the Jitra Line—at a cost of twenty-seven dead. The Japanese had captured more than 3,000 British and Malayan defenders.

Yamashita questioned captured officers. They told him that British commander General Arthur Percival had decided to bunch his best troops on the island of Singapore hoping the Japanese could not cross the water and capture the naval base. To Yamashita, such a strategy sounded like the thinking of a frightened, already-defeated enemy.

DECEMBER 11: *Manila, MacArthur's headquarters*

Puffing on his corncob pipe, MacArthur listened on the phone to field commanders reporting that Japanese troops were landing at four beaches on this island of Luzon. "The landings are only jabs to draw our forces to the wrong places," MacArthur told his commanders. "The main attack is yet to come. When it does, the main landings will be at Lingayen Gulf."

MacArthur knew that the gulf's shallow waters and broad beaches were ideal for landing troops from the sea. MacArthur's father, also an American general, had landed an invading army at Lingayen Gulf some forty years earlier to defeat Filipino rebels.

The island of Luzon, with its seaport of Manila, was the key to conquering all of the Philippines. The American War Department plan was known as War Plan Orange. It called for the defenders of Luzon to fall back to the mountainous jungle peninsula of Bataan, which was protected at its tip by Corregidor, an underground fortress carved into rock. War Plan Orange calculated that the defenders could hold out on Bataan and Corregidor for six months. Then the Navy would arrive, bombard the enemy, and land reinforcements to rescue Bataan's defenders.

MacArthur brushed aside WPO's fall-back strategy as "defeatist." He was confident that his troops could stand, fight, and as he had told reporters months earlier, "throw any attackers into the sea."

DECEMBER 11: *Berlin, the Kroll Opera House*

Members of the Reichstag, the German lawmakers who passed Hitler's laws, glanced uneasily at each other as Hitler walked onto the stage. His face was more pasty-white than usual, mouth drawn tight, jaw tense. The Reichstag members guessed the news from the Russian front was especially bad.

The crowd in the balconies of the huge hall hushed as Hitler began to speak. Roosevelt had gone mad, he said, and forced Japan to go to war. He asked the Reichstag to put Germany side by side with its Axis partner. The members voted to declare war against the United States.

DECEMBER 12: *Near Smolensk*

G uderian watched from a hillside as Russian troops and tanks pierced his lines. He had talked by radio with the other commanders of the three armies that had attacked Moscow. Fresh Siberian troops were ramming into the middle of the German line across Russia. If the Russians smashed through, they could loop around and trap the Germans. The generals knew they had to stop the frantic flight of their armies—but they also knew their soldiers were too sick, exhausted, cold, and hungry to turn around and fight.

What-ifs kept buzzing in Guderian's head. *What if* Hitler had not postponed Barbarossa in favor of Operation Punishment? Guderian's tanks would have rolled across the flat plains stretching in front of Moscow in the dry warmth of summer instead of in winter's rain and snow.

And *what if* Hitler had not turned Guderian's tanks south last month? *What if* his tanks had kept driving toward Moscow? Would the German armies now be warming their feet in

front of Moscow fireplaces? Guderian told himself that he and other German generals would
debate those questions the rest of their lives.

DECEMBER 20: *A Luzon beach*

MacArthur drove up to the front in his
dusty Packard limousine. He could hear
the jabber of rifles and machine guns. His
80,000 troops—15,000 Americans and 65,000
Filipinos—had thrown back the Japanese invaders, as he had pledged they would. MacArthur
knew the victories had been won against lightly
armed landing parties—but, finally, Americans
had won a battle in this two-week-old war.

DECEMBER 21: *Manila, MacArthur's headquarters*

Warehouses on Luzon were filled with
canned food that could keep Mac-
Arthur's army fed through at least four years of
fighting. Supply officers wanted to truck that
food to the safety of Bataan and Corregidor.
But MacArthur needed the trucks to whisk
troops to wherever the Japanese might land on
Luzon. The food stayed in the warehouses.

DECEMBER 22: *Aboard HMS* Battleship Duke of
York, *Hampton Roads, Virginia*

Churchill paced his cabin, anxious for the
warship to dock. As soon as he had
learned of Pearl Harbor, he told himself he
must cross the Atlantic to confer again with
Roosevelt. He feared America would turn its

might toward the Pacific, eager to avenge the attack on Pearl Harbor. "They may concentrate on Japan," he told a British general, "and leave us to deal with Germany."

DECEMBER 22: *Lingayen Gulf, Luzon*

As General Homma watched from his flagship two miles offshore, his 40,000 troops—Manchurian coal miners who had fought for years in China—stormed ashore. Battleships and cruisers lobbed shells that smashed concrete forts along the shore. The grizzled Japanese veterans sprayed shells from automatic weapons at Filipino scouts carrying single-shot Enfield rifles. The scouts fled, "vanishing into the hills," one commander reported to MacArthur.

Homma's China veterans swung down Route 3 toward Manila no more than a hundred miles away.

DECEMBER 23: *The Luzon plains*

Looking "like a tired hawk," as one of his officers put it, the sixty-one-year-old MacArthur stared through binoculars at the advancing Japanese columns. He realized that General Homma was trying to swallow

Japanese soldiers raise high their battle flags shortly after landing in the Philippines. Most had fought for years in China, and rated the Chinese soldiers almost as tough as themselves. But, after two weeks of fighting against the Americans, Japanese soldiers told a Japanese reporter that the Americans fought as fiercely as the Chinese. *(National Archives)* his two armies—the North Luzon Force and the South Luzon Force—inside rapidly closing jaws. The Japanese invaders were not going to be thrown into the sea.

MacArthur radioed new orders to his commanders: "War Plan Orange is in effect." Both forces should retreat to Bataan before they were caught in Homma's trap.

DECEMBER 23: *The White House Cabinet Room*

R oosevelt and Churchill sat at the end of the conference table. British generals and admirals sat on one side, American military men on the other side.

"We believe," Churchill began hesitantly, "that Germany must be destroyed first, and only then should we turn to win in the Pacific."

Roosevelt did not blink. "Of course," he said, "Hitler first, Japan second."

Churchill took his cigar out of his mouth, surprised. "No argument?"

"No argument at all," the President said.

America's Army and Navy chiefs of staff, General Marshall and Admiral Harold (Dolly) Stark, glanced at each other. They often said that the British were capable of asking for the moon—and Roosevelt would give it to them. In the months ahead, they suspected, there would be many arguments about how much of America's strength should go to Europe and how much would go to her besieged armies and navies in the Pacific. But all the Americans agreed: Germany must be defeated first. Japan would then be cut off from fuel for its war machinery and defeated.

DECEMBER 23: *Wake Island, the Pacific*

Since the first Japanese air raid on December 8, Major Jim Devereux and his 378 Marines had fought off an invasion force of destroyers and cruisers. The Marines' artillery had already sunk two destroyers and set a light cruiser aflame. Like MacArthur, Devereux hoped to fight until the Navy came to rescue him.

Wake sat midway between Pearl Harbor and Japan, a natural air and naval bastion to protect sea avenues to Japan. The Marines knew how badly the Japanese wanted the island. The Marines mowed down waves of landing parties charging up from beaches all over the island. "If they want this island," Corporal Hershal Miller screamed during one battle on the beach, "they gotta pay for it."

Lieutenant Robert Hanna crouched in his foxhole, dazed after two weeks of continual fighting with only snatches of sleep. As dawn's light crept across the ocean, he saw a destroyer slipping close to the shore, crammed with Japanese soldiers. Hanna dashed to an antiaircraft gun and began to load and fire the gun all by himself. The ack-ack shells crashed into the destroyer's crowded deck. Flames burst around screaming, wounded, mangled soldiers. Other

Marines ran to the shore and sprayed the decks with machine guns. Within minutes, the white surf crashing on the beach had turned into red froth.

The phone was ringing in Major Devereux's command post. Twenty Marines, he was told, had been wiped out by two bursts from a Japanese destroyer. A messenger from another outpost stumbled into the dugout, gasping, "They're killing 'em all."

His band of Marines had fought for sixteen days, lost almost a hundred dead and wounded while killing hundreds of Japanese and sinking or damaging four warships. But for the first time, Devereux was thinking of surrender. His phone rang again. A Navy commander told him that Japanese soldiers were creeping over the entire island. The lives of 1,200 American civilians, who had been workers on the island, could no longer be protected. "I guess," said the commander, "we'd better give it to them."

Devereux said to a sergeant, "Fix up a white flag and pass the word to cease firing."

Carrying the white flag on a broomstick, Devereux walked down to the beach where a Japanese officer awaited him. Devereux walked by dirty-faced, bandaged Marines who were passing the word: "Major's orders . . . we're surrendering . . ." On a suddenly hushed island, two Marines stood at a flagpole near the beach and began to lower the Stars and Stripes.

DECEMBER 25: *Manila, MacArthur's headquarters*

"Stand and fight, slip back, dynamite," MacArthur was instructing his best commander, the tall and gaunt Brigadier General Jonathan (Skinny) Wainwright. "Then stand and fight, slip back, dynamite."

MacArthur wanted General Wainwright to delay the Japanese with bullets and blown bridges while he attempted a "double retrograde." His North and South Forces were now two columns that were marching almost a hundred miles apart. Like a chess master moving his pieces on a board, MacArthur was trying to move the two forces backward and sideways at the same time so they could slip through one funnel into Bataan.

Peering at a map, MacArthur's bony finger pointed to bridges that Wainwright had to blow up as he retreated. MacArthur knew every jungle trail in Luzon. He had charted those trails forty years earlier as a second lieutenant just out of West Point.

His finger stopped at Calumpit Bridge, twenty miles north of Manila. He told Wainwright that his men had to hold that bridge against Japanese attackers until every last soldier of the two forces had crossed safely into Bataan.

DECEMBER 25: *Wolf's Lair*

No Christmas decorations hung from rafters in the gloomy, shedlike headquarters. The German army's new commander in

German officers question a Russian prisoner who stands behind the barbed wire of a POW camp. Many Russian prisoners, and civilians, were eager to join the German army during the early months of the war. They wanted to overthrow Stalin's dictatorship. But, once they saw the horrors of Nazi barbarism, Russians joined partisan bands that killed Germans behind the front lines. *(National Archives)*

chief, Adolf Hitler, was conferring with General Halder. A week earlier, Hitler had accepted General von Brauchitsch's resignation. Hitler told Halder that the former commander in chief was a "nincompoop" who had cost Germany more than a million casualties so far in the invasion of Russia. Of every three Germans who had crossed into Russia, one had been killed, wounded, or treated for frostbite.

"This little matter" of being commander in chief, Hitler told Halder, "is something anyone can do. I know of no general who could do [what] I want . . . done."

What he wanted—no, demanded!—was a halt to the retreat. "Dig in," he exhorted Guderian by telephone. "I forbid further withdrawals!"

One of Hitler's shrewdest strategists, General Guenther Blumentritt, later told Guderian, "Hitler's fanatical order that the troops must hold fast . . . was undoubtedly correct." The troops were fleeing across open, snow-covered hillsides, wide open to the cross fire of ambushing Siberian ski troops. To survive, they had to stop and seek cover to shoot back.

Within a week, Hitler had gotten rid of his top generals. Guderian, von Rundstedt, and von Bock quit or were fired. Hitler dismissed hundreds of generals and colonels, sending some to military prisons and later to firing squads.

"The front will remain where it is regardless" of how many men are killed, Hitler instructed a commander, General Werner von Tippelskirch.

The short, stumpy von Tippelskirch glowered angrily as he listened to Hitler. But Hitler's do-or-die order steeled German units to stop, dig in, and fight on a front now 200 miles from Moscow. Years later, Tippelskirch wrote that Hitler's "order not to retreat was his one great achievement . . ." If the panicky retreat had gone on much longer, he said, Hitler's legions would have been slaughtered before they got to the Russian border.

But General Halder knew that a mighty change had taken place. The year 1941 had come to an end with the German juggernaut now on the defense for the first time in this two-year-old war. "The myth of the invincibility of the German army," he told his diary, "was broken."

DECEMBER 28: *Manila, Homma's headquarters*

Homma bit his lip, angry and frustrated. He had captured Manila but lost MacArthur's army.

"His soldiers are running in panic to Bataan," an aide told Homma.

"Not so," Homma growled, staring at a map showing troop movements. "They are retreating as he has planned it. He is attempting a double retrograde, and so far he has done it brilliantly. He will try to cross his forces at the Calumpit Bridge."

Homma ordered tanks and troops to converge at the bridge. "Capture it or destroy it," Homma ordered. "But don't let the Americans cross it."

DECEMBER 29: *Calumpit Bridge*

Skinny Wainwright stood on a slope on the Bataan side, and watched thousands of weary American and Filipino troops tramp across the bridge. Trucks, buses, and horse-drawn wagons also crossed, carrying the sick and wounded.

Wainwright had massed his riflemen and machine gunners to guard the far side of the bridge. Their guns faced the jungle and the Japanese tanks they knew were coming.

DECEMBER 31: *Calumpit Bridge*

The fidgety Wainwright glanced at his watch. It was close to five o'clock in the evening. MacArthur had told him to blow up the bridge at 6 P.M. MacArthur feared the Japanese would seize the bridge, opening a door to Bataan. But Wainwright worried that American stragglers might still be making their way through the jungle.

Lieutenant Dan Petree, a twenty-five-year-old Army tank commander, peered through the firing slots in his light tank. He saw the column of Japanese tanks lumber out of the jungle, their guns aiming at the bridge. Petree rammed his tank forward, his machine guns spewing .50-caliber armor-piercing bullets.

One Japanese tank exploded, a red ball outlined against the dusky green jungle. Two other American tanks crossed the road leading to the bridge, red sparks flying from their muzzles.

The Japanese tanks scurried back into the jungle. American and Filipino troops ran out of hiding places to race across the bridge.

Chapter Thirteen

JANUARY 1, 1942: *Calumpit Bridge*

Dawn's first light broke across the jungle treetops as Wainwright looked at his watch for the tenth time in thirty minutes. It was a little after 6 A.M., more than twelve hours after MacArthur's deadline for blowing the bridge. Wainwright saw Japanese tanks, with infantry moving stealthily behind them, creep out toward the bridge.

He ordered his troops and tanks to hurry across the bridge to the Bataan side. As the last tanks rumbled by him, Wainwright turned to engineer Bob Casey and said curtly, "Blow it!" Calumpit Bridge blew up in the faces of swearing Japanese officers.

Wainwright jumped into an old Chevrolet and rode toward Bataan's mountains and jungles. He knew that most of the trucks that had jounced across Calumpit had been empty. MacArthur had switched to War Plan Orange so quickly that his supply officers didn't have time to load food from the Army's filled warehouses. The warehouses had held enough food to feed a Bataan army for years, but now they

IMPORTANT AIR-RAID WARNING!

Passengers and crews are now required by law to leave street cars, buses and trackless trolleys and seek shelter, under penalty of fine, imprisonment or both. Conductors and operators will issue upon request special Air Raid Slips, good as fares on any vehicl... ...to one-half hour after the second "Blue" signal.

As the new year of 1942 drew nearer, Americans worried that their cities would be bombed by Japanese or German planes as London and Pearl Harbor had been bombed. This warning was posted on all buses in Baltimore. (*Library of Congress*)

were feeding the Japanese. MacArthur would have to put his tired, hungry troops on half-rations—thirty ounces of food a day.

JANUARY 1, 1942: *Washington, the White House, a second-floor bathroom*

Churchill and Roosevelt had talked late into the night on New Year's Eve about how twenty-six nations had joined the United States, England, and Russia to declare war on Germany, Japan, and Italy. Churchill and Roosevelt had tried and failed to think up one name for the twenty-nine allies.

It was only eight in the morning of New Year's Day, but Roosevelt guessed that Churchill might be awake. He rolled his wheelchair into Churchill's bedroom. A surprised butler told him that the Prime Minister was· in his bath.

Roosevelt rolled to the bathroom door, knocked, then threw open the door. Churchill stared at the President from a bathtub filled with steaming hot water, his chest pink, a cigar sticking jauntily out of the side of his mouth.

"Winston," Roosevelt said, "how about this name: the United Nations?"

The Prime Minister slowly took the cigar out of his mouth. "That ought to do it," Churchill said.

A closer look at

CHURCHILL

HIROHITO

HITLER

ROMMEL

ROOSEVELT

STALIN

TOJO

YAMAMOTO

WINSTON
CHURCHILL

1874–1965

Winston Spencer Churchill caught the eyes of Britishers from his earliest years as a bold and dashing soldier, journalist, and author. During World War I, he led the British navy as its First Lord of the Admiralty. Churchill's popularity dropped during the Depression of the 1930s. He was rich and a conservative. Unemployed Englishmen thought that conservatives did not do enough to help them find jobs. But when Allied armies collapsed in early 1940, political leaders asked him to become prime minister. In 1940 and 1941, he inspired the English with ringing speeches. He took control of the army and navy, dictating strategy to generals and admirals. He wanted to beat Hitler and he wanted to keep the British Empire intact as a global power. He often made military moves that were important both in winning the war and in securing land and natural resources needed by his island-based empire. And he worked day and night to convince America to join the fight against Hitler.

EMPEROR
HIROHITO
1901–1989

I n the presence of an emperor regarded as a
god, even the crusty Japanese general, Hideki Tojo, felt his knees wobble when a
faint look of displeasure crossed the Emperor's face. Hirohito ascended to his father's
throne in 1926. In 1931, the Japanese began to
expand the Empire of the Rising Sun by conquering China's Manchuria. In 1937, they attacked China to acquire more land and natural
resources. The Emperor did not forbid these
land grabs by the military. Like the military, he
believed the growing population of Japan could
survive only by moving to larger lands. But
late in 1941, he forced the military to think
twice before becoming embroiled in World War
II. He hinted strongly to them that diplomacy
be tried before reaching for the sword. He approved a face-to-face meeting between his
prime minister and Roosevelt, and the offering
of compromises to Washington. Roosevelt decided against the meeting and turned down
deals that included handing over China to Japan. A quiet-spoken man who liked poetry,
Emperor Hirohito questioned pilots after the
Pearl Harbor attack and wanted to be assured
that no hospitals, schools, or places for civilians
had been bombed.

ADOLF
HITLER
1889–1945

itler grew up in Linz, Austria, the
son of a border guard for the Aus-
tro-Hungarian government. As a
teenager, Adolf went to Vienna to
attend an art academy, but he was rejected as
untalented. Humiliated, he became a homeless
person, living in Vienna's slums. When World
War I began in 1914, he joined the German
army. He blamed Germany's defeat on Jews
and Communists who "stabbed Germany in
the back." In the 1920s, he joined the new Nazi
party. His fiery anti-Communist and anti-
Semitic speeches were believed by the defeated
Germans. He rose to become Germany's chancellor in 1933, and built up the German army.
He demanded more "breathing space" for Germany's "cooped-up" millions. He bullied Europe's war-weary leaders. They stood aside as
he grabbed land, including his native Austria.
But after he attacked Poland in 1939, World War
II broke out. His generals feared their outnumbered armies would quickly lose. When his
troops, spearheaded by tanks and planes, shattered the poorly prepared Allied armies, they
began to bow to his every command.

ERWIN ROMMEL

1891–1944

The son of an impoverished schoolteacher, Erwin Rommel grew up in an army in which most generals were wealthy Prussian noblemen. Machines fascinated him, and he became an expert on the strategic use of tanks and armored cars, commanding what the Germans would make famous as Panzer (armored) troops. He argued to older officers that modern battles would be won by armies hitting with speed and surprise. The stocky, blue-eyed Rommel caught Hitler's attention in 1940 during the conquest of France. Leading his tanks and armored cars at the front, Rommel used speed and daring to surprise and trap millions of Allied soldiers. He was contemptuous of Hitler's top generals, at one point, snapping at General Halder: "What did you ever do in war apart from sit on your backside in an office?" In 1941, Hitler sent Field Marshal Rommel to North Africa to help the Italians capture Egypt and the Suez Canal. Rommel organized the Afrika Korps, whose tanks would advance, retreat, and advance again during two years of bloody battling on the desert sands of Libya and Egypt.

FRANKLIN DELANO ROOSEVELT

1882–1945

The son of a wealthy New York State merchant, Roosevelt graduated from Harvard and became a lawyer in New York City. He ran for Congress in 1912 and soon became one of New York's most popular Democrats. He served in World War I as assistant secretary of the navy, and ran for vice president in 1920. He and his running mate, James Cox, lost. Soon after, he was stricken by infantile paralysis and remained in a wheelchair the rest of his life. His popularity never waned, however, and in 1932 he was elected President. He would become the first and only President to serve a third term and win a fourth. He steered the country out of the depths of the Great Depression. He despised dictatorships and sought to defeat Hitler. But he knew Americans did not want war. From 1939 to the attack on Pearl Harbor, he sought ways—some legal, some illegal—to help Great Britain.

JOSEF STALIN

1879–1953

S tudying to be an Orthodox priest when he was fifteen, Josef Stalin—"Sosso" to his adoring mother—instead became a revolutionary. To get money for his Communist Bolshevik Party, he planned bank robberies. He was imprisoned eight times by the czarist government from 1903 to 1917. After the czar was deposed, Stalin became the right-hand man of the communist leader Nikolai Lenin, and in 1922 he was elected general secretary of the Communist Party. In Moscow, people said, "Lenin trusts Stalin, but Stalin trusts no one." He expanded his power after Lenin's death, executing thousands of revolutionary leaders during the "Purge Trials" of the 1930s. In 1939, he shocked the world by signing a nonaggression pact with Hitler, who had sworn to destroy communism. Stalin had brushed away Churchill's pleas to join England in the war against Hitler, but after Hitler attacked Russia, Stalin demanded help from England and America. Much to the annoyance of Churchill, who disliked the crude, vodka-swilling dictator, Roosevelt was delighted by his rough ways and began to call him "Uncle Joe."

HIDEKI TOJO
1884–1948

A general who believed strongly that Japan's swelling population could survive only by taking land on the Asian mainland, Tojo became Japan's war minister in the early 1930s. When the emperor decided in October of 1941 that Japan should try diplomacy to avoid war, Japan's military men picked Tojo to be prime minister. A bold general, they thought, would show the United States that Japan would go to war if diplomacy failed. His appointment, however, dismayed more sophisticated Japanese, such as Admiral Yamamoto, who said, "Even though he is bold, he doesn't know the background of the situation and he will be unable to improve matters." Honest and hardworking, Tojo began to have serious doubts that Japan could win the war as the attack on Pearl Harbor approached. He put pressure on his envoys in Washington to make a deal with Roosevelt, but he and the military would not give up their dream of acquiring the vastness of China. Churchill heard that America was considering giving China to Japan, and urged Roosevelt not to do so. Roosevelt agreed. That broke up peace talks in Washington. Tojo then approved the signal to his fleets approaching Pearl Harbor and Southeast Asia to begin the war.

171

ISOROKU YAMAMOTO
1884–1943

He was born Isoroku Takano, but was adopted by the Yamamoto family in 1916, when he was thirty-two, because the Yamamotos had no male heir and wanted the family name to continue. Short (five-foot-three), with square shoulders and a thick chest, Yamamoto never learned how to fly airplanes. But in 1924, he took command of Japan's first flight school for naval pilots. He came to America in the late 1920s as a naval attaché with the Japanese Embassy in Washington. He studied at Harvard. He realized better than most Japanese the immense size of the United States. In the late 1930s, he wrote bitingly about the foolishness of "the armchair arguments about war by our politicians." In 1939, he became commander in chief of the Japanese Combined Fleet. In 1940, he began his plan to attack America's Pacific Fleet at Pearl Harbor. The crippled fleet, he theorized, could not ship troops to attack Japan in the Philippines and Southeast Asia until the Japanese were dug in too deeply to be driven out. The brilliance of his 1941 strike would be dimmed by his decisions that led to the 1942 Battle of Midway in the Pacific.

WORLD WAR II
CHRONOLOGY FOR 1941

Jan. 1, Bulgaria agrees to allow German troops to cross its territory to attack Greece. King Paul and other Yugoslavian leaders decide to sign the Tripartite Pact, joining the Axis. **Jan. 5,** British Army of the Nile takes Bardia in Libya, North Africa, and forces the Italians to retreat toward the Libyan port of Tobruk. **Jan. 10,** Lend-Lease bill is introduced in U.S. Congress. **Jan. 22,** British capture Tobruk. **Jan. 29,** British and American military and diplomatic delegates meet secretly in Washington and discuss global strategy in the event the United States goes to war against Germany and Japan.

Feb. 10, Prime Minister Churchill orders the Army of the Nile to send troops from Egypt to aid Greece if Germany joins Italy in attacking Greece. **Feb. 12,** General Rommel begins to organize the Afrika Korps in Libya to join the Italians. **Feb. 17,** Turkey agrees to allow German troops to cross Bulgaria. The agreement dims Churchill's hopes that Turkey will join the war against the Axis powers.

Mar. 6, Churchill issues his Battle of the Atlantic Directive, reorganizing air and sea forces to improve the guarding of convoys bound for Britain. **Mar. 11,** President Roosevelt signs the Lend-Lease bill into law. Great Britain can buy weapons and food from America and pay for them after the war. **Mar. 16–17,** A new secret weapon, radar, helps to sink two German U-boats. **Mar. 25,** Yugoslavian leaders sign the Tripartite Pact and join the Axis. **Mar. 27,** Yugoslavian air force officers lead a popular revolt and depose King Paul. Tripartite Pact is rejected. Seventeen-year-old Prince Peter becomes the new king. Hitler orders an attack on Yugoslavia and Greece and postpones Operation Barbarossa, his attack on Russia that had been scheduled for May 15. **Mar. 31,** Rommel attacks the British at Libya's Mersa Brega and forces a headlong retreat by the British across Libya toward Tobruk and Egypt.

APRIL

Apr. 6, Germany invades Yugoslavia and Greece, where British troops and planes have arrived from Egypt to join the Greeks. **Apr. 11,** Roosevelt sets up the Office of Price Administration (OPA) to hold down rising prices caused by the demand for war goods by the American and British armed forces. **Apr. 13,** Russia and Japan sign a five-year agreement not to go to war against each other. The agreement is welcomed in Tokyo because it frees Japan to plunge southward without fearing a stab in its back from Russia in the north. **Apr. 19,** British troops begin to evacuate Greece as some Greek armies surrender to the Germans. **Apr. 29,** Germany completes its conquest of Yugoslavia and Greece. **Apr. 29,** Rommel begins a frenzied series of attacks on Tobruk, where Australians and New Zealanders are entrenched after the retreat across Libya. Tobruk must be captured by Rommel if his tanks are to roll into nearby Egypt and capture Cairo and the Suez Canal. But the Tobruk defenders throw back eight days of attack and Berlin orders Rommel to stop attacking and try to starve out the defenders.

MAY

May 10, One of Reich Chancellor Hitler's closest Nazi Party leaders, Rudolf Hess, flies to Britain in a small plane to try to talk the British into making peace with Germany. Hitler says that Hess has no authority to negotiate peace. The British imprison Hess. He will spend the rest of his life in Allied jails. **May 10–11,** A heavy German air attack on London damages the Houses of Parliament. It is the heaviest bombing of a British city of the war—but it will be the last big attack on London for three years. Hitler is shifting his air armadas eastward to Russia. **May 20,** German paratroopers land on the Mediterranean island of Crete, held by the British and Greeks. The Germans conquer Crete in two weeks. Hitler's air general, Hermann Göring, boasts that "no island is safe" from Hitler's blitzkriegs. **May 20,** A U.S. merchant ship, the *Robin Moor,* is sunk by a German torpedo in the South Atlantic. Roosevelt calls the sinking an "act of intimidation" by Hitler, but admits that the ship carried war supplies to Britain. **May 27,** British warships sink the German battleship, *Bismarck,* in the Atlantic 700 miles off France.

JUNE

June 1, British and Free French troops capture the capital of Iraq, which had been seized by pro-Axis forces. **June 8,** Other Free French and British troops invade Syria, held by the German-dominated French government. The Free French are commanded by General Charles de Gaulle. **June 15,** General Wavell's Army of the Nile launches Operation Battleaxe to free the Tobruk defenders, but the British tanks are stopped by German guns. An angry Churchill decides to replace Wavell. **June 22,** Three million German and other Axis troops invade Russia and plunge amost 300 miles into Russia in the first week. **June 30,** General Claude Auchinleck replaces Wavell as the British commander in Africa.

JULY

July 3, At the Imperial Conference, Japan's military and political leaders discuss with Emperor Hirohito their plans to seize Southeast Asian colonies owned by the British, the

French, and the Dutch. The Emperor is told that Japan should risk war with the United States and England to get those rich lands. **July 10–11,** Roosevelt asks Congress for more than $8 billion to build up America's Army and Navy. **July 11,** Free French and British troops accept the surrender of the Vichy (German-dominated) French army in Syria. **July 12,** For the first time, German planes bomb Moscow. **July 16,** Hitler designates Martin Bormann and Alfred Rosenberg to supervise the "elimination" of Jews and commissars (Communist Party leaders) in Russia. **July 26,** Roosevelt appoints Lieutenant General Douglas MacArthur, a retired chief of staff of the U.S. Army, as the commander of American and Filipino forces in the Philippines. **July 26,** Roosevelt and the Dutch East Indies government begin to take measures to cut off oil to Japan, which had been getting 90 percent of its oil for its army and navy from those two sources. **July 28,** The French Vichy government allows Japan to occupy bases at Saigon and Hanoi in French Indochina. The bases put Japan within easy range of the British naval bastion at Singapore in Malaya.

AUGUST

Aug. 5, The Germans smash their way into Smolensk, killing or capturing more than half a million Russian defenders. The Germans are only about 200 miles from Moscow. **Aug. 9–12,** Churchill and Roosevelt meet at sea off Newfoundland. They issue what is called the Atlantic Charter, stating that no nation should be dominated by another. **Aug. 12,** A bill to extend the Army service of draftees from twelve months to thirty months passes the House by a vote of 203–202 and is signed into law by the President. **Aug. 23,** At Hitler's direction, the main thrust of the German invaders of Russia turns south to capture Kiev in the oil- and grain-rich Ukraine. **Aug. 30,** Germans surround the Russian city of Leningrad. Almost a million civilians and defenders face slow starvation.

SEPTEMBER

Sept. 1, By order of Reinhard Heydrich, a chief German security officer, all Jews in Europe over the age of six must wear the yellow Star of David badge to show publicly that they are Jewish. Experiments continue at the Auschwitz concentration camp on use of gas to exterminate large numbers of people. **Sept. 4,** The U.S. destroyer *Greer* is attacked by a German U-boat. The *Greer* attacks the U-boat, which escapes. **Sept. 11,** Roosevelt orders U.S. warships to "shoot on sight" any foreign warship in waters that American ships are patrolling "for American defense." **Sept. 19,** Kiev falls to the Germans, the Russians losing half a million in the battle, the Germans about 100,000. The Germans turn their tanks northward to mass for a final assault on Moscow. **Sept. 24,** Fifteen nations join the United States, England, the Free French, and Russia in signing the Atlantic Charter, the cornerstone of what would later be called the United Nations.

OCTOBER

Oct. 2, Operation Typhoon, the German attack on Moscow, officially begins with the German spearheads about 120 miles from the capital. **Oct. 8,** In a series of battle about 100 miles from Moscow, the Germans capture or kill almost 600,000 Russians and seize millions of tanks and guns. **Oct. 15,** German security officers decree that any Jew found outside a Polish ghetto will be immediately executed. **Oct. 16,** Foreign diplomats, Russian government workers, and Communist Party leaders begin to flee Moscow by train and car. The new provisional capital will be Kuibyshev, more than 600 miles southeast of Moscow. **Oct. 16,** War Minister Tojo takes the place of a diplomat, Prince Konoe, as prime minister. **Oct. 31,** The U.S. destroyer *Reuben James* is sunk by a German U-boat in the North Atlantic. One hundred of the crew perish.

NOVEMBER

Nov. 5, Tojo's government decides on new peace proposals to be sent to the United States. **Nov. 7–8,** Almost 400 British bombers raid Berlin and other German cities. The British lose thirty-seven planes. The high losses during these nightly raids—and their slight impact on German morale and factories—causes Churchill to stop the attacks until spring. **Nov. 18,** The British Army of the Nile in North Africa has been reorganized as the Eighth Army under General Auchinleck. The Eighth Army begins Operation Crusader to free the defenders of Tobruk. **Nov. 20–25,** Japan's envoys offer the new Japanese peace offers to the United States and get counteroffers. **Nov. 22,** British and German tanks and infantry fight in the desert between Tobruk and the Egyptian border. **Nov. 23,** German troops come to within thirty-five miles of Moscow. **Nov. 25–26,** A Japanese naval task force that includes six aircraft carriers slips out of Japan to sail toward Pearl Harbor. Troopships and battleships mass in Japanese ports to sail southward. **Nov. 30,** The United States makes clear to Japan that Japan must not try to expand into Southeast Asia. Japan's Tojo tells other political leaders that peace talks in Washington are not succeeding.

DECEMBER

Dec. 2, A coded message is flashed to the Pearl Harbor task force from Tokyo: Begin the war. **Dec. 2,** German troops bed down in a suburb within sight of the Kremlin less than twenty miles away. **Dec. 6,** The Russians throw a major counteroffensive at the Germans massed around Moscow, spearheaded by a million fresh Siberian troops, and the Germans begin a panicky retreat. **Dec. 7,** More than 300 planes from the Japanese task force bomb Pearl Harbor. **Dec. 7,** Japanese troops swarm into British Malaya and attack the British colony of Hong Kong. **Dec. 7,** Japanese planes attack Clark

Field near Manila. **Dec. 7,** Japan declares war on Great Britain and the United States. **Dec. 8,** America declares war on Japan. **Dec. 8–11,** Rommel has lost so many tanks in fighting with the Eighth Army that he must retreat and give up the siege of Tobruk. **Dec. 10,** Japanese troops land on Luzon, where Manila is located. **Dec. 11,** Germany and Italy declare war on the United States. **Dec. 19,** Hitler takes over as commander in chief of his armies as the German retreat in Russia continues. **Dec. 21–23,** Main Japanese invasion army lands on Luzon and is soon within a hundred miles of Manila. **Dec. 22,** Churchill arrives in Washington. He and Roosevelt agree that Germany will be defeated first, then Japan. **Dec. 23,** At Wake Island in the Pacific, U.S. marines surrender to a Japanese naval task force after more than a week of fighting. **Dec. 25,** The Japanese capture Hong Kong. **Dec. 27,** General MacArthur's two Luzon armies retreat toward the jungle peninsula of Bataan. **Dec. 31–Jan. 1,** MacArthur's forces complete the withdrawal into Bataan. **Dec. 31,** Russians recapture Tula, 150 miles south of Moscow.

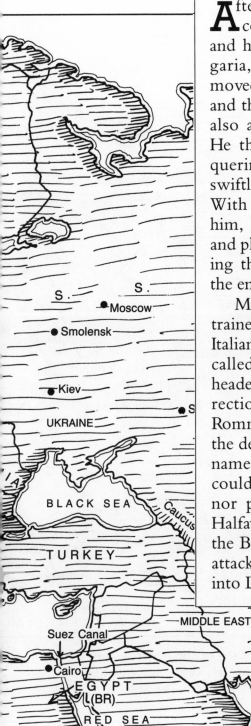

After sweeping eastward to conquer Poland, Hitler and his Axis allies (Italy, Bulgaria, Rumania, and Finland) moved on to France, Belgium, and the Netherlands, which he also attacked and conquered. He then traveled south, conquering Yugoslavia and then, swiftly and decisively, Greece. With those successes behind him, he turned eastward again and plunged into Russia, reaching the gates of Moscow near the end of the year.

Meanwhile, the specially trained tank corps made up of Italian and German soldiers and called the Afrika Korps was headed for Egypt under the direction of General Rommel. Rommel's brilliant strategies in the desert earned him the nickname the Desert Fox, but he could neither capture Tobruk nor push the British beyond Halfaya Pass. It was there that the British rallied and counterattacked, driving Rommel back into Libya.

This map shows the arms of the Japanese war plan. One arm would thrust westward to capture the Philippines, the "front door" to the rest of Southeast Asia. With the front door locked, the arm would continue westward with little fear of being attacked from its rear as it conquered Borneo, the Celebes, and the rest of the Dutch East Indies, as well as British Burma, British Malaya, and its naval base at Singapore, plus French Indochina (later to become Vietnam). Japan would then be

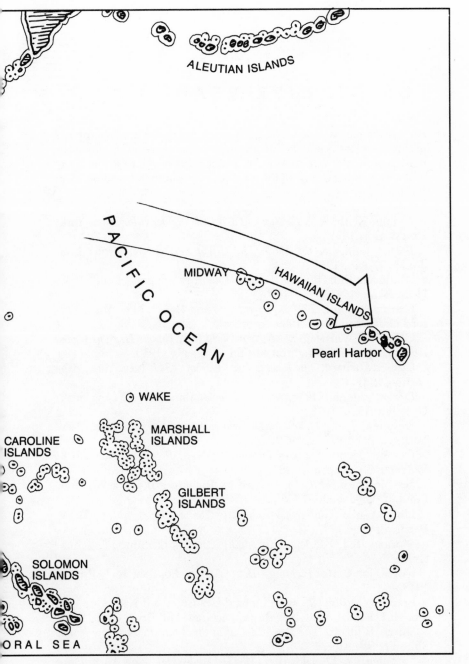

ALEUTIAN ISLANDS

PACIFIC OCEAN

MIDWAY

HAWAIIAN ISLANDS

Pearl Harbor

⊙ WAKE

MARSHALL
ISLANDS

CAROLINE
ISLANDS

GILBERT
ISLANDS

SOLOMON
ISLANDS

ORAL SEA

poised to strike at India and hook up with German armies coming from the Middle East and Russia. The second arm of the Japanese military would strike eastward
to capture islands like Guam, Wake, and the Solomon,
Gilbert, and Marshall islands, some 2,000 miles from
Tokyo. Those islands would be launching pads for attacks to capture Hawaii and land troops on America's
West Coast. Those bases would also be used to attack
southward and conquer New Guinea and then Australia.

FOR FURTHER READING

All of the material, including quotations and dialogue, that appears in this book has been taken from magazine articles and books written about World War II. For the reader who wants to know more of the events that occurred during 1941, I recommend reading from this list:

Ayling, Keith, *R.A.F.: Story of a British Fighter Pilot,* New York, Holt & Co., 1941.

Batten, John, *Call the Watch: The Men of the Merchant Marine,* London, P. Davies, 1942.

Beauman, Eric, *Winged Warriors: Our Airmen Speak,* London, W. Heinemann, 1941.

Campbell, John, *The Experience of World War II,* New York, Oxford University Press, 1989.

Churchill, Winston, *The Second World War, Volume III, The Grand Alliance,* Boston, Houghton Mifflin Company, 1950.

Collier, Richard, *The Road to Pearl Harbor: 1941,* New York, Atheneum, 1981.

Devaney, John, *Hitler, Mad Dictator of World War II,* New York, G. P. Putnam's, 1978.

Devaney, John, *Douglas MacArthur: Something of a Hero,* New York, G. P. Putnam's, 1979.

Devaney, John, *Franklin Delano Roosevelt, President,* New York, Walker and Company, 1987.

Fest, Joachim, *Hitler,* translated by Richard and Clara Winston, London, Weidenfeld & Co., 1974.

Long, Gavin, *MacArthur, Military Commander,* London, B. T. Batsford, 1969.

Morgan, Ted, *F.D.R.: A Biography,* New York, Simon & Schuster, 1985.

North, John, *Men Fighting—Battle Stories,* London, R. P. Prince, 1948.

Prange, Gordon W., with Donald Goldstein and Katherine Dillon, *At Dawn We Slept,* New York, McGraw-Hill Book Co., 1981.

Shirer, William, *The Rise and Fall of the Third Reich,* New York, Simon & Schuster, 1960.

Sommerville, Donald, *World War II Day by Day,* New York, Dorset Press, 1989.

Time-Life Book Editors, *The Luftwaffe,* New York, Time-Life Books, 1982.

Zieser, Benno, *In Their Shallow Graves,* translated by Alec Brown, London, Elek Books, 1956.

1942: AMERICA FIGHTS THE TIDE

THE YEAR 1941 ENDED WITH AMERICA REELING BACKWARD AFTER SUFFERING THE WORST NAVAL DEFEAT IN ITS HISTORY. THE NEW YEAR WOULD BE ONLY A FEW MONTHS OLD WHEN AMERICANS FELT THE STING OF THE WORST MILITARY DEFEAT IN THEIR HISTORY—THE SURRENDER OF GENERAL MACARTHUR'S ARMIES IN THE PHILIPPINES.

AS THE JAPANESE SWEPT SOUTH AND WEST TOWARD THE BORDER OF INDIA, THE ALLIES BEGAN TO FEAR THAT THE JAPANESE AND GERMANS WOULD HOOK UP TO ENCIRCLE HALF THE GLOBE. IN THE PACIFIC AND INDIAN OCEANS, JAPANESE PLANES AND SHIPS SANK BRITISH AND AMERICAN BATTLESHIPS.

HITLER'S ARMIES IN EUROPE RETURNED TO THEIR ATTACK IN RUSSIA, AND THE RUSSIANS FELL BACK SLOWLY AND STUBBORNLY, LOSING MILLIONS MORE OF THEIR POORLY TRAINED TROOPS. IN AFRICA, GENERAL ROMMEL SPRANG AT THE BRITISH AND SOON STOOD AT THE GATES OF CAIRO AND THE SUEZ CANAL.

AGAIN, AS IN 1939, 1940, AND 1941, THE AXIS TIDE SEEMED UNSTOPPABLE. BUT IN 1942 THE FIGHTING MEN OF AMERICA, CANADA, AUSTRALIA, NEW ZEALAND, RUSSIA, AND ENGLAND WOULD SHOW AT FOUR PLACES SCATTERED AROUND THE GLOBE THAT THE TIDE COULD BE STOPPED. THE FOUR PLACES WERE CALLED EL ALAMEIN, MIDWAY, STALINGRAD, AND GUADALCANAL.

INDEX

Afrika Korps, 53, 60, 74, 147, 168
America. *See* United States of America
Australia, 53
Austria, 167

Barbarossa 18, 46, 72
Bataan, 149, 151, 156, 159–61
Battle of Britain, 7, 9–13, 25, 36–38
Bulgaria, 51, 56, 78

Canada, 12
Chiang Kai-shek, 6
China, 6, 166
Chronology of major events, 173–79
Churchill, Winston, 4, 7–8, 19–20, 30–31, 53, 71, 73, 89–90, 151–53, 162–63, 165, 170, 171
Communists, 58, 72, 87, 167, 170

Cox, James, 169
Czechoslovakia, 56

De Gaulle, Charles, 66
Denmark, 56

Egypt, 23, 33, 53, 55, 168
Eire, 12
England. *See* Great Britain

Finland, 78
France, 2, 8, 56, 58, 84
Free French, 66, 74
Fuchida, Mitsuo, 118–19, 127–28, 131, 140

Genda, Minoru, 116, 118, 127, 140
Germany, 1, 2–3, 7, 32, 39, 51–52, 56, 58, 60–61, 65, 67–69, 71, 78–79, 115, 124, 149–51, 167, 168
Great Britain, 2–4, 7, 14, 17, 21, 39–40, 58, 64, 74–75, 84, 165, 169, 170

Greece, 24, 30–31, 32, 39, 43, 46, 51, 53, 55, 56, 74
Guderian, Hans, 91–92, 98, 100–101, 109, 124–25, 150, 157–58

Hirohito, Emperor, 83, 166
Hitler, Adolf, 1–4, 7, 17–18, 23–25, 30–31, 43–44, 51, 57–59, 62, 64, 67, 71–72, 74, 79–81, 83, 85, 88, 91–92, 95, 98, 125, 149–50, 157–58, 165, 167, 168, 170
Holland. See Netherlands
Homma, Masaharu, 107–8, 152–53, 159
Hopkins, Harry, 19–20, 89, 121, 141
Hull, Cordell, 85, 112–13, 120, 127–28, 141–42
Hungary, 56

Italy, 23–24, 30, 39, 51–52, 78, 168

Japan, 5–6, 18, 21, 39, 49, 83, 141, 166, 171, 172
Jews, persecution of, 34, 58, 62, 72, 93–94, 99–103

Kennedy, John F., 23
Kennedy, Joseph P., 22–23, 31
Khrushchev, Nikita, 80–82, 85
Kretschmer, Otto, 34–35, 40–42

Kurusu, Saburo, 108, 112–14, 120, 126, 141

Lend-Lease, 17–18, 20–23, 39
Lenin, Nikolai, 170
Libya, 23, 30, 32, 44, 52, 74, 168
Luxembourg, 56

MacArthur, Douglas, 144–46, 148, 151–53, 156, 159–61
Marshall, George, 112–14, 153
Mussolini, Benito, 23–24, 30, 49, 55, 81

Nagumo, Chuichi, 109, 117, 127, 140
Netherlands, 38, 56, 84
New Zealand, 53
Nomura, Kichisaburo, 84, 114, 120, 126, 128, 141

Pearl Harbor, 21–22, 76–77, 96–97, 117, 120, 126–40, 145, 151–52, 166, 169, 171, 172
Philippines, 49, 90, 145–46, 148, 156–61, 172
Poland, 1, 2, 56, 66, 167
Prien, Gunther, 34–36

Rommel, Erwin, 32–33, 44–45, 52–53, 60, 74–75, 147, 168
Roosevelt, Franklin D., 6, 13–14, 16–18, 20, 30, 39,

Roosevelt, Franklin D. *(cont'd)*
46–47, 81, 85, 88–90, 95,
114, 121, 141–44, 160,
162–63, 166, 169, 170,
171, 172
Rumania, 51, 56
Russia. *See* Union of Soviet
Socialist Republics
(USSR)

Schepke, Joachim, 34–35, 40–
41
S.S. (Schutzstaffel, or Black-
shirts), 1, 72, 87
Stalin, Josef, 3, 18, 49, 57–58,
71, 73–74, 79–81, 85–86,
99, 105, 170
Stewart, Jimmy, 42

Timoshenko, Semin, 79
Tobruk, 45, 53, 62, 64, 75,
147
Tojo, Hideki, 83, 104, 115,
166, 171

Union of Soviet Socialist Re-

publics (USSR), 44, 46,
71, 73, 86, 91–92, 116,
121–24
United Kingdom. *See* Great
Britain
United Nations, 163
United States of America, 5,
6, 14, 17–18, 21, 43, 49,
58, 141, 150, 165, 166,
169, 170, 171, 172

Wainwright, Jonathan, 156,
159–61
Wake Island, 154–55

Yamamoto, Isoroku, 21–22,
76–77, 96–97, 108, 110,
118–19, 171, 172
Yamashita, Tomoyuki, 107–8,
115, 147–48
Yugoslavia, 43–44, 46–52, 55–
56

Zhukov, Georgi, 79, 105,
124–25
Zieser, Benno, 110–12, 125